"James said to her, "Let this flower, my dear Mary, be the emblem of humility and sweetness, by its modest color, its disposition to flourish in hidden places, and the delicate perfume which it sends forth. May you, my dear child, be like the violet, modest in your demeanor, careless of gaudy clothing, and seeking to do good without making any fuss about it."

The Basket of Flowers

GREAT CHRISTIAN BOOKS

LINDENHURST, NEW YORK

PUBLISHER'S NOTE REGARDING ITS RIGHTS WITH RESPECT TO THIS EDITION

The Basket of Flowers

CHRISTOF VON SCHMID

Great Christian Books

is an imprint of Rotolo Media
160 37th Street Lindenhurst, New York 11757,

ISBN 978-1-61010-049-6

Johann Christoph von Schmid, 1768-1854,
A Basket of Flowers / by Christoph von Schmid
p. cm.
A "A Great Christian Book" book
GREAT CHRISTIAN BOOKS an imprint of Rotolo Media
978-1-61010-049-6,
Recommended Dewey Decimal Classifications: 200, 240
Suggested Subject Headings:
1. Religion—Christianity literature—Historical Fiction
2. Christianity—Fiction—Devotional
I. Title

Book and cover design are by Michael Rotolo, www.michaelrotolo.com. This book is typeset in the Minion typeface by Adobe Inc. and is quality-manufactured on acid-free paper stock. To discuss the publication of your Christian manuscript or out-of-print book, please contact us.

Manufactured in the United States of America

Contents

Chapter One

THE GARDENER'S DAUGHTER

THE story which is related in the following little book happened long ago, in a country the manners and customs of which are in many respects different from ours. This will account for some things in it which might otherwise seem strange and improbable. Two things, however, will be found the same through every difference of time and place—two principles which have constantly been acting in opposition to each other from the earliest period of the world's history. On the one hand, we find the sinful human heart the same in all ages, producing what the Bible calls "the works of the flesh," and leading to misery unutterable; and, on the other hand, the remedy for this evil, in the work of the Holy Spirit of God, producing what the Bible calls the "fruits of the Spirit," and leading as surely to perfect happiness and peace. In this little story the working of these opposing principles, and the fruits brought forth by each, may be easily traced; and as we are all partakers of the same evil natures, to be sanctified and saved, if saved at all, by the same Holy Spirit, we may all profit by studying the working of these in the experience of others, however their outward circumstances may differ from ours.

In the little village of Eichbourg in Germany, there lived, about a hundred years ago, a very worthy man, whose name was James Rode. When James was quite young, he was sent to learn to be a gardener in the beautiful gardens of the Castle of Eichbourg. He was a poor orphan, little cared for at that time by anyone, poorly clothed and scantily fed, and obliged to work very hard, for the Count of Eichbourg's gardener was a rigorous taskmaster. Despite the arduous conditions James was happy. Though poor, he was rich; he possessed a treasure more precious than gold or silver. He had been the child of many prayers; carefully instructed by a pious father and mother; and his heart had been early touched by God's grace. Piety is lovely in all, but more especially in the young, when the new nature is implanted in the heart before the evil passions have had time to grow strong, and the inward struggle becomes hard and difficult. The fruits of the Spirit were early seen in the character and conduct of James, and attracted the notice and admiration even of those who did not understand whence they proceeded. Gentle and obedient, always diligent at his work, ready to oblige; possessing the natural politeness that flows from a kindly heart, and the bright sunny cheerfulness produced by a contented mind and a conscience at ease, James soon became a general favorite. He was often invited into the castle, and sometimes permitted to share in the instructions given to the children of the Count; and when the young Count, having finished his education, was sent to travel, James was chosen to accompany him as his attendant.

In this situation he diligently made use of all the means of improvement within his reach. By the grace of God in his heart, he was preserved amid the many temptations by which he was now surrounded, and he became daily more a favorite with his master; so that, on his return to Eichbourg, after having fulfilled his engagement, the Count offered him an honorable and lucrative employment in his household, in the magnificent palace which he possessed in Vienna.

James was now compelled to make a choice, something like that set before Lot when he chose to go and live in Sodom, because it was in a well-watered and pleasant land. In the Count's household God was not honored, and James knew that he would there be required to do many things contrary to his conscience. He therefore declined the honorable and lucrative situation offered him, and preferred returning to the humble labor from which he had been taken. The Count willingly gave him a lease, on easy terms, of a small piece of ground near Eichbourg. This little domain consisted of a pretty cottage, an orchard well planted with fruit trees, and a large kitchen garden. Shortly after he took possession of it, James married Anne, whose principles, feelings, and tastes, were like his own; and they lived comfortably in their pleasant cottage through the sale of the vegetables and fruit they grew.

Many pleasant years passed smoothly and happily by. God blessed James and Anne with children sent to enliven their cottage; and for a season they enjoyed the purest earthly happiness. But God, who chastens even his best-loved children, will not suffer them to become too deeply attached to the things of this world. Afflictions are sent to remind them that this world is not their rest—to wean their affections from earth, and fix them above. It pleased God to take back to himself one after another of their children, thus gradually loosening earthly ties. Then came, for James, the last and severest blow of all—for after a sudden and brief illness his beloved Anne followed her children. One daughter was mercifully left in his care; and in this beloved child he invested all his care and affection.

She was a beautiful child, and his precious Mary grew; daily becoming more engaging. Her father's instructions and prayers seemed to have been blessed to her, for she appeared to grow in goodness while she grew in stature. When she was only fifteen, she was able to take the entire charge of her father's house. Never was there a more amiable or more useful girl. Their little dwelling was managed with the utmost of proficiency—proving always a pattern of neatness and order; not a trace of dust was to be seen in it, and the kitchen utensils shone as if they had just come from the shop. Her father's indoor comforts were all attended to, yet Mary found time to help him in his work in the garden. The hours thus spent were the happiest of her life. She had grown up among the flowers, and she loved them as those only can, who watch their growth and cultivate them with their own hands. Her father fostered and indulged this taste by procuring for her the rarest seeds and flower roots. These were well cared for, and anxiously watched by Mary. Her flowers were her friends and companions; she waited impatiently for the opening of the first bud of every new kind, and if its beauty equaled her expectations, she eagerly flew to her father to tell him of her new treasure. James smiled at her delight, and rejoiced to see her satisfied with such innocent pleasures. "How many men," said he, "lavish much more money in gay dresses and ornaments for their children than I spend in flower seeds, without procuring for them half the enjoyment that Mary feels in her flowers! Then this enjoyment is of so much superior a kind. The love of dress and ornament degrades the taste, and renders the character frivolous; but the love of flowers, rightly directed, enriches both the intellect and the heart."

James's garden became celebrated for its beauty in all the neighborhood. Few could pass that way without stopping to admire it; the village children as they passed from school, peeped through the hedge, or stood lingering by the little gate; and Mary seldom failed to give them some pretty nosegays to carry home, or a few seeds or roots to plant in their own little gardens.

James took advantage of his daughter's love for flowers, to give her many lessons of heavenly wisdom. Often he used to say, "Let others spend their money for jewels and silks and other adornments; I will spend mine for flower-seeds. Silks and satins and jewels cannot procure for our children so pure a pleasure as these beautiful exhibitions of the wisdom and benevolence of God."

He found... "religious meanings in the forms of nature." (Coleridge)

He knew that... "the beauties of nature are not given for our amusement or enjoyment merely, but for our education and instruction;" that ours is a disciplinary world, and that the lessons of nature are a part of God's own discipline with us." (Cheever)

He felt how near we are to God in every part of his creation, when "alive unto God through Jesus Christ our Lord." (Rom. 6:11b)

He had the keen spiritual eye which can discern the Creator in his works, and read the blessed messages He thus sends to his children, and the clear and enlightened faith which thus holds communion with God.

> *"One spirit, His,*
> *Who wore the plaited crown with bleeding brows,*
> *Rules universal nature. Not a flower*
> *But shows some touch, in freckle, streak, or stain,*
> *Of his unrivaled pencil. He inspires*
> *Their balmy odors, and imparts their hues,*
> *And bathes their eyes with nectar, and includes*
> *In grains as countless as the seaside sands*
> *The forms with which he sprinkles all the earth.*
> *Happy who walks with Him! whom what he finds*
> *Of flavor or of scent in fruit or flower,*
> *Or what he views of beautiful or grand*
> *In nature, from the broad majestic oak*
> *To the green blade that twinkles in the sun,*
> *Prompts with remembrance of a present God."*

—COWPER'S TASK

James was accustomed to devote the first morning hours of every day to meditation and prayer, and in order to save time for this, he rose before the dawn. He felt that no one can live as a Christian who does not endeavor to save the first hour, or even half hour in the morning, for communion with God. In the fine summer mornings, Mary often accompanied him to a little arbor which commanded a beautiful view of the garden, and of the rich and lovely country round. Here he taught his beloved child, and prayed with her, and here he found a text for his lessons in every surrounding object. Pointing to the bright rays of the rising sun, he spoke to her of the Sun of Righteousness; he explained to her the darkness of her heart by nature, and the Source of light and life; he pointed out the lessons taught in Scripture from the rain and from the dew; he made her listen to the praises of God in the morning song of the birds. He endeavored to teach her trust in God, who clothes the lilies and feeds the birds, though they sow not, nor reap, nor gather into barns. He read with her the parables of the sower and the seed, the wheat and the tares, the small grain of mustard seed, similes pertaining to the kingdom of heaven, the barren fig-tree and the vineyard. He spoke to her of the first garden where man was placed, and of his sad expulsion from it,—of the garden as the emblem of her own soul, given her to cultivate, and to bring forth fruit to God, of the garden as the emblem of the church of God, in which Jesus himself delights (Canticles 4:12,16; 5:1; 6:2), where his people flourish as trees of righteousness, the planting of the Lord; and of the glorious garden above, to which, in his own good time, God transplants his people, through which flows the river of the water of life, and in which is the tree which bears twelve manner of fruits, whose leaves are for the healing of the nations.

In the beauty of the various flowers which adorned their garden, in the charming variety of their shapes, in the perfection of their proportions, in the glory of their colors, and in the sweetness of their perfumes, he taught Mary to see and admire the power and wisdom and goodness of God. It was his custom to begin each day with God by spending the first hours of the morning in prayer; and, in order to accomplish this without neglecting his work, it was his habit to rise early. In the beautiful days of spring and summer, James would lead Mary to an arbor in the garden, and, while the birds sang their joyous songs, and the dew sparkled on the grass and flowers, he delighted to talk with his daughter of God, whose bounty sent the sun and the dew, and brought forth the beauty and life of the world. It was here that he first instilled into Mary's mind the idea of God as the tender Father of mankind, whose love was manifested not only in all the beautiful works of nature, which were round them, but above all in the gift of Jesus Christ. It was in this arbor that James had the happiness of seeing Mary's heart gradually unfold to the reception of the truth.

He explained to her the blessed hope of the resurrection of the body, taught to us by the springing of the seed (1 Cor. 15:35-38). But above all, he loved to trace the Saviour in the various emblems under which he is presented to us in Scripture, as the Root of David (Rev. 22:16), the Branch of Righteousness (Zech..3:8), the First-Fruits of them that sleep (1 Cor. 15:20), the Plant of Renown (Ezek. 34:29), the Rose of Sharon (Canticles 2:1), the Fountain, the Sun, the Bright and Morning Star. Kneeling by her father's side, Mary learned to pray— no formal prayer, but as she heard her father pray, from the very depths of his heart. The first hours of the morning thus spent were very profitable to the little girl, and contributed much, by the blessing of God, to the education both of her mind and of her heart. Mary's favorite flowers were the violet, the lily, and the rose, and James loved to find in them emblems of the graces of the mind, which he wished her to cultivate.

Once in the early part of March, when with shining eyes and bounding feet she brought him the first violet, James said to her, "Let this flower, my dear Mary, be the emblem of humility and sweetness, by its modest color, its disposition to flourish in hidden places, and the delicate perfume which it sends forth. May you, my dear child, be like the violet, modest in your demeanor, careless of gaudy clothing, and seeking to do good without making any fuss about it. In its quiet dress of deep blue, decked by no gaudy colors, it modestly hides under the green leaves and is scarcely seen, while shedding around it a fragrant perfume. Try to emulate it, my dear Mary; do not overly value your outward appearance, to concern oneself with gaudy clothing, but strive to obtain that 'ornament of a meek and quiet spirit, which is in the sight of God of great price.'"

Mary's father then made a bouquet of lilies and roses, and, giving it to Mary, he said, "These are brothers and sisters, whose beauty no other flowers can equal. Innocence and modesty are twin sisters, which cannot be separated. Yes, my dear child, God in His goodness has given to modesty, innocence for a sister and companion, in order that she might be warned of the approach of danger. Be always modest, and you will be always virtuous. Oh, if the will of God be so, I pray that you may be enabled to preserve in your heart the purity of the lily!"

In the season when the lilies and roses were in full bloom and when the garden was resplendent with beautiful flowers, the old man, seeing his daughter filled with joy, pointed to a lily unfolding in the rays of the morning sun. "See, in this lily, my daughter, the symbol of purity. Its leaves are finer than richest satin, and its whiteness equals that of the driven snow. Happy is the daughter whose heart also is pure, for remember the words, 'The pure in heart shall see God.' The more pure the color, the more difficult to preserve its purity. The slightest spot can stain the flower of the lily, and so one word can rob the mind of its purity.

Scarcely can they be touched when they are injured. Thus the very least approach of vice pollutes and corrupts the soul. Pray, dear Mary, for purity of heart. Remember that though polluted by nature, we may nevertheless be washed free from stain in the Fountain opened for sin and for uncleanness, and that God has promised that though 'our sins are red as crimson, they shall be white as snow.' None but the pure in heart shall see God; none but those washed and clothed in the spotless white robe of Christ's righteousness shall ever sit down at the marriage-supper of the Lamb.

And then he went on to say, "Let the rose," he said, "be the emblem of modesty, as it resembles the blush which rises to the cheek of a modest girl. But there is another lesson to be learned from the rose: after its beautiful colors have faded, it still retains its fragrance; when its leaves are brown and withered, they are even sweeter than in their fresh and lovely youth. Thus is it, dear Mary, with a true Christian. Thus let it be with you. The cheek of youth will fade, outward beauty will decay, but strive to acquire those graces of the mind which are unfading and imperishable."

One ornament of their garden, which James and his daughter most dearly prized, was a dwarf apple-tree little higher than a rose-bush, which grew in a small round bed in the middle of the garden. The old man had planted it on his daughter's birthday, and every year it gave them a harvest of beautiful golden yellow apples spotted with red. One season it seemed specially promising, and its blossom was more luxurious than ever. Every morning Mary examined it with new delight. One morning she came as usual, but what a change had taken place! The frost had withered all the flowers, which were now brown and yellow and fast being shriveled up by the sun. Poor Mary's sensitive feelings were so affected that she burst into tears, but her father turned the incident to good account.

"Look, my child," said he, "as the frost spoils the apple-blossoms, so wicked pleasures spoil the beauty of youth. Oh, my dear Mary, tremble at the thought of going aside from the path of right. If the time should ever come when the delightful hopes which I have had for your future should vanish, I should shed tears more bitter than you do now. I should not enjoy another hour of pleasure, and my gray hairs would be brought with sorrow to the grave." At the mere thought of such a calamity the old man could not keep back his tears, and his words of tender solicitude made a deep impression on Mary's heart. Thus did she daily learn from her good old father to use the eyes of her mind, as well as her bodily eyes, and to see in the beautiful things around her, the lessons they were intended to teach. Nurtured under the care of so wise and loving a father, thus Mary grew up like the flowers of her garden, fresh as the rose, pure like the lily, modest as the violet, and full of promise for the future, as a beautiful shrub in the time of flourishing.

When James viewed his beautiful garden, with its luxuriant flowers and its prolific fruits, which so well repaid his constant care, it was with a feeling of satisfaction and gratitude. But this feeling was nothing compared with the joy he felt when he saw his daughter, as the reward of his pious efforts to train her in the love of God, bringing forth the most precious fruits of the Holy Spirit.

"Here he might lie on fern or withered heath,
While from the singing lark, that sings unseen
The minstrelsy that solitude loves best;
And from the sun, and from the breezy air,
Sweet influences trembled o'er his frame;
And he, with many feelings, many thoughts,
Made up a meditative joy, and found
Religious meanings in the forms of nature.
And so, his senses gradually wrapt
In a half sleep, he dreams of better worlds;
And dreaming hears thee still, Oh singing lark
That singest like an angel in the clouds."

COLERIDGE—*Tears in Solitude*

[Have you, who read this little book, thus learned to use your eyes? Do you know that the eyes of your mind are naturally darkened, so that you can neither read with understanding the book of nature, or the book of God's word. When David prays, Open mine eyes, that I may see wonderful things out of thy law," he speaks of the eyes of the mind, which must be opened before the Bible can be rightly understood; and in the same way we must pray to God to open our eyes before we can see him in his works, and learn the lessons he has inscribed upon them. If your eyes are not yet opened, young readers, you are losing a rich source of pleasure, as well as profit. Pray to God to open them, and then go into the free air, with the Bible for your interpreter, and read the lessons that Mary read. Listen to hear the still small voice that speaks from among the birds and the flowers, and if you once hear it, you will find the enjoyment so sweet, you will ever wish to hear it again, you will love it more than can be told, you will wonder at your former blindness.]

Chapter Two

THE BASKET OF FLOWERS

ONE fine morning, in the beginning of May, Mary went into the woods to cut some willows and twigs of hazel for her father's work, as he was accustomed to employ himself in his leisure hours in making ornamental baskets, of various kinds, for James was an industrious man, who liked to be constantly busy. He knew that we are commanded in the Bible to "redeem the time." After Mary had cut the willows, she found a beautiful bed of lilies of the valley. She gathered a large bunch, and tied them up into two neatly arranged bouquets, one for her father, and one for herself. She then proceeded homeward by a narrow footpath through the woods. She had not gone far when she crossed paths with the Countess of Eichbourg and her beautiful red-haired daughter Amelia, who had lately returned to the castle from their residence in the capital. Mary, who possessed that native politeness which is natural to a sweet and gentle spirit, stepped modestly aside, to allow the ladies to pass, curtsying respectfully at the same time.

"Oh, what beautiful lilies of the valley," exclaimed the young Countess, who loved flowers passionately, and preferred wildflowers to any other kind.

On hearing this exclamation, Mary offered a bouquet to each of the ladies. They received them with pleasure, and the Countess, taking out a silk purse richly embroidered with gold, offered some money to Mary, but she refused to accept a penny.

"Oh no, no, my lady," said she, "I cannot take money for my flowers. My father and I have received many benefits from the Count. Please permit a poor girl to have the pleasure of offering you this little gift without being paid for it."

The Countess smiled pleasantly, and said, Well, my child, will you be so kind as sometimes to bring a bunch of lilies of the valley to the castle for my daughter?"

Mary promised to do so; and every morning, as long as the lilies of the valley lasted, she carried a beautiful bunch to the castle.

The young Countess Amelia was charmed with the flowers; and she became very fond of Mary. She often invited her to return to the castle after the season of lilies was past, and frequently kept her there for hours. Their tastes were similar in some respects, especially in their mutual love of flowers, which gave them always a common subject of interest, and they became much attached to each other.

By and by, when Amelia's birthday drew near Mary wished to give her a little rustic present. She had taken her so many bouquets, that she tried to think of something more uncommon for a birthday gift. During the previous winter, her father had made several very pretty baskets. He had given the prettiest of them to Mary. She asked permission to give this basket to the young Countess. He willingly consented; but even further improved the gift, by weaving on the basket, in very delicate workmanship, the letters of the Countess Amelia's name, and the crest of her family. When finished, the basket was quite an exquisite masterpiece.

On the morning of Amelia's birthday, Mary gathered her finest roses and superb stocks—white, red, and purple. She added to these a variety of flowers of every color, so tastefully arranged among the fresh green leaves, that the effect was absolutely elegant. Round the edge of the basket, she wove a delicate wreath of rosebuds and moss. The letters of Amelia's name were surrounded by a coronet of forget-me-nots. The mixture of the rosebuds, the delicate hue of the forget-me-nots, and the fresh green moss, looked very pretty against the pure white basket-work. It was certainly a gift worthy of an aristocrat. Even the ever serious James was pleased; and when Mary was going to take it away, he said, "Leave it a few minutes longer—I like to look at it."

At length, Mary carried the basket to the castle, and presented it to the young Countess, with many sincere wishes for her happiness. Amelia was charmed with the basket. She could not find words to express her delight and admiration.

"You are too kind, my dear Mary," said she; "you must have ransacked your little garden to bring me such a profusion of flowers. And how beautiful the basket! It does great credit to your father's skill. I have never seen anything so exquisite, its shape is so elegant. Come with me to show it to mamma.'

Saying these words, the young Countess took Mary by the hand, and running up the staircase which led to the Countess's room, she entered hastily, leading in Mary, and exclaiming, as she opened the door, "Oh mamma, mamma, look what a beautiful present Mary has brought me! Is it not exquisite? I am sure you have never seen a more elegant basket or lovelier flowers."

The Countess admired the basket extremely, "It is indeed charming," said she; "it is beautifully arranged; I would like to have a painting made from it. The basket, the flowers, the fresh dew-drops still glittering among them, would make an admirable study for a flower-painter. The whole does infinite credit to the taste and kind feeling of this good little girl. Wait here a moment, my child," said she to Mary, making a sign at the same time to Amelia to follow her into the next room, and thus leaving Mary alone. "We cannot allow this child to go away," said the Countess to her daughter, "without giving her some present for her trouble: what do you propose to give her?"

Amelia thought a moment, and then said, "I should like to give her one of my dresses, mamma, if you will allow me to do so. I think the dress, with red and white embroidered flowers on the dark green fabric, would be the best. It is almost new. I have only had it on once or twice; but as I have grown of late, it is now too short for me. Mary is not as tall; it will fit her just fine, and will serve as a nice Sabbath dress for her. If you approve of my idea, I would like to give it to her."

"Very well," replied the Countess, "it is always best to give something that is useful. It will be an appropriate present too. The green dress, with red and white flowers, will be very suitable for the darling flower-girl."

The Countess then returned to her room with Amelia, and looking kindly at Mary, she said, "Go now, children, carry off this charming basket, and take care that the flowers do not fade before dinner is served. There will be a large party at dinner today, and the basket will be the most beautiful ornament on the table. Good-bye, little Mary, I shall leave Amelia to thank you for your pretty gift."

Amelia hastened to return to her own room and asked Margaret her lady's-maid to bring her the green dress but in an uncharacteristic manner Margaret hesitated to obey. "Does your ladyship wish to wear that dress?" she asked. "No," replied Amelia, "I intend to give it to Mary."

"Give it to Mary?" blurted Margaret. "Is the Countess aware of this?"

"You forget yourself strangely, Margaret," said Amelia, in a grave tone; "do as I request of you immediately, without your opinion, and bring me the dress now."

"Certainly my lady!" Margaret responded, and left the room hastily to hide both her displeasure and her reddening cheeks due to the reprimand she had received from the young Countess. Her face was on fire; she crumpled more than one of the young Countess's dresses in her anger, before pulling out from the wardrobe the one requested.

"Oh, if I dared, I would tear it to pieces," muttered she; "that horrid flower-girl! I truly hate her! She has already taken my place in the Countess Amelia's favor, and now she steals this dress from me, steals it, for *I* ought to have *all* the dresses that the Countess no longer wants. Oh, how I truly hate her! I will be revenged of her." Margaret, however, found it prudent to keep her displeasure to herself, and suppressing it as she best could, she reappeared with a feigned smile upon her otherwise impudent face, and presented the green dress to her mistress.

"My dear Mary," said Amelia, "I have received many more valuable gifts than your's today, but not one which has given me so much pleasure. The flowers on this dress are not nearly so pretty as yours, but I hope that you will wear them for my sake. Think of me when you put on this dress; and, pray, present my compliments and thanks to your father."

Mary received the dress, thanked the young lady, and took leave of her, as it was getting late, and Amelia must begin to dress. Margaret was called to assist her, and it was with difficulty that she suppressed the outward expression of the evil temper she was indulging. Notwithstanding her efforts to conceal it, she could not altogether succeed; and Amelia perceived, from the way in which her hair was roughly handled, that her maid's temper was disturbed.

"What is the matter, Margaret?" said she; "are you angry because I gave Mary that dress? Haven't I given you several?"

"It would be very foolish in me, my lady, to be angry simply because your ladyship chooses to be generous," replied Margaret cleverly, although she was still roiling inwardly.

"That is a sensible speech," said the young lady; "but I hope, Margaret, that you really feel what you say."

In the meantime, Mary had reached the cottage, and hastened to display her new dress to her father. But this costly present did not please the wise old man. He shook his head gravely, and said, "I almost wish, my dear Mary, that you had not taken the basket to the castle. The dress is valuable, certainly, as a gift from the young lady; but I fear that it may cause us to be envied by our neighbors; and, what would be still worse, I fear it could make you vain. Be on your guard, dear Mary. I hope you will never learn to be overly fond of dress. Remember what the Scripture says about the true ornaments of woman."

[Reader, Do you appreciate stylish clothing and accessories? It's important to recognize that an obsession with fashion, accessories, jewelry, makeup and hairstyles can reflect a lack of depth and maturity. When someone is overly concerned with their looks and adornment, it often reveals an inner focus on superficiality rather than true beauty.

Embrace the elegance of simplicity. By cultivating a refined taste through an appreciation of nature and meaningful pursuits, you can move beyond the fleeting allure of trends that many find appealing.

It's worth noting that a preoccupation with external appearances can lead to negative consequences. This fixation may set individuals on a troubling path, potentially resulting in poor choices or harmful behaviors.

Parents should be vigilant if they notice their children developing an excessive desire for materialistic fashion. Rather than encouraging this mindset, it's crucial to guide them towards more substantial interests, much like addressing early signs of a health issue. True beauty lies in authenticity and self-acceptance rather than in outward appearances.]

Chapter Three

THE COUNTESS'S RING GOES MISSING

IMMEDIATELY after Mary left the castle the Countess Amelia noticed that a precious diamond ring, which she remembered having put down on her worktable, in the room where Mary was left alone for a few minutes, was missing. As no one had been in that room but Mary, suspicion naturally fell on her. The young Countess was deeply grieved at this, and entreated her mother to conceal the loss for a time, and to allow her to go herself to the cottage, and persuade Mary to return the ring, if she had really been tempted to take it, and so to save her from exposure and disgrace.

Mary had just folded up the new dress, and put it away in her drawer, when she heard a hasty step in the garden, and the young Countess appeared, quite out of breath, with anxiety and distress pictured in her face.

"Oh, Mary!" exclaimed she, "my mother has lost a diamond ring. No one was in the room when she left it but you. They suspect you—they accuse you of having taken it. Is it possible you can have done so? If you have been tempted to do it, dear Mary, give it back to me. I will excuse you to mamma. No one shall ever know anything of it—only give me back the ring."

Mary, completely taken by surprise, could at first scarcely comprehend Amelia's words. "What can you mean, my dear young lady?" said she, "I have no ring. I saw no ring in the room where I was. I touched nothing. I never even moved from the place where I was sitting."

"Mary, Mary," said Amelia, earnestly, "I implore you to tell me the truth. You do not know what a serious matter this is. The stone in that ring alone cost more than a thousand crowns. If you had known this, you would not have touched it, I am sure. Perhaps you thought it was only a trifle, of no consequence. Oh, dear Mary, if you have touched it, do confess it, and it will be forgiven, as an act of childish thoughtlessness."

Mary at length comprehended the full horror of the suspicion which had fallen upon her. Pale as death, and trembling all over, her feelings were too deep for tears. "Indeed, my lady," said she, "I know nothing whatever of your ring. I have never in my life even ventured to touch what was not mine. How can you suppose that I would take even a trifle? My father early taught me not to take even a pin that belonged to another."

At this moment, James entered the room. He had seen the Countess Amelia pass hastily through the garden alone. This unusual visit, her look of agitation and haste, had made him suspect that something was wrong. He hastened to the cottage. "What has happened?" he said, as he entered.

At the answer to his question, the good old man became so agitated that he was forced to lean against the table for support. "Mary, my dear child," said he, "remember that the theft of a ring of this value is, by the laws of this country, punishable with death. But this is not the worst. Think of God's commandment, 'Thou shalt not steal.' A crime, such as theft, brings upon the offender not only punishment by human laws, but what is much more dreadful, the anger of the Almighty and Omniscient God, who sees the heart, and cannot be deceived by lies or excuses of any kind. If you have so far forgotten God, my poor child, as to be guilty of the crime of which you are accused, if you have suffered yourself to be tempted by the glitter of gold and jewels, do not now increase your sin by denying it. Confess your guilt, and restore the ring! This is now the only means of averting a part at least of the consequences of your crime. Alas! that I should ever have to speak so to you."

These words redoubled Mary's agony. "Oh, my father, my father," said she, can *you* believe me guilty? Need I assure you that I have never seen the ring. You surely know that if I had even found a ring of this value on the road, I could not have rested till I had restored it to its owner. Indeed, indeed, I have not the ring."

"I hope you are telling the truth, Mary," said James, in a severe tone. "This good young lady seems unwilling to accuse you, but the evidence against you is strong. She has kindly come here to try to save you from disgrace. She deserves that you should be sincere with her. Oh Mary, be candid, tell the whole truth."

"Oh, my father," said Mary, "you know that I never stole a farthing in my life.

I have never even gathered an apple from a tree that was not yours, or pulled a flower in a neighbor's garden without permission. I have never even seen the ring. This is the simple truth. Have I ever told you a lie in my life, my dear father? You know I have not—how can you doubt me now?"

James still persevered. He was anxious to try his daughter to the uttermost. "My child," said he, "do not bring my gray hairs with sorrow to the grave. Spare me the agony of seeing you persist in sin. I ask you, solemnly, as in the presence of God, who sees your heart, before whom you must one day appear, tell me if you have the ring. I implore you to consider well, and to speak the truth."

Mary raised her eyes, now bathed in tears, and, clasping her hands, she said, solemnly, "God is my witness that I have not the ring. He sees my heart. In His presence, I say to you, I am speaking the very truth. I have not the ring I have not even seen it."

"Well," said her father, "I do believe you, my child. You have not stolen the ring. I know that if you had, you could not deny it so solemnly. I feel that you are speaking the truth. And since this is the case, since you are innocent, dear Mary, I feel uneasy no longer. Be calm, my dear child, and fear nothing. There is only one evil to be feared in this world, and that is sin. Prison and death are nothing compared to a guilty conscience. If we are destined to suffer unjustly, if all the world forsake us, God will not forsake us. In Him we shall find a friend, a comforter, and sooner or later He will make manifest our innocence."

The Countess Amelia's tears were flowing fast at these words. She wiped them hastily away, and said, "When I hear your pious words, when I see Mary's look of innocence, I believe you are speaking truth—I believe that you have never seen this unfortunate ring. But when I remember all the circumstances of the case, I know not what to think. Where can it be? Mamma remembers distinctly laying it on the work-table, near the window, in the room where Mary was left alone. No one else was there, except mamma, Mary, and me. Mary herself will remember that I never went near the side of the room where the table stood. There is no entrance to that room, without passing through mamma's, which she had never left when she missed the ring. Instead of ringing for her maid to look for it, mamma herself searched every part of the room carefully, more than once. She admitted no one, not even me, until she was quite sure that the ring was not to be found in the room."

"I cannot explain this," said Mary's father. "It is a mystery to me as well as to you. God has sent us a severe trial, but it is well. His will be done." The good old man raised his eyes to Heaven, and said, "Oh Lord, we are thine, do with us as Thou wilt; only grant us, we pray thee, grace and strength to bear the trials that it may please thee to send."

"Alas!" said Amelia, weeping bitterly, "what can be done? How shall I go home without the ring? I can do nothing to help you. Mamma has not yet told anyone of the loss, but she cannot conceal it long. Papa will be home before dinner. If mamma has not on that ring, he will observe it immediately. He gave it to her at my birth, and she has always been accustomed to wear it on my birthday. He will miss it he will insist on knowing where it is. Mamma must tell all. I do believe you innocent, dear Mary. I will assure them of it: but how shall I make them believe me?"

The amiable Amelia left the cottage with a sad heart and tearful eyes. Mary scarcely moved to bid her farewell, she could not speak, she seemed frozen with grief. James sat down by the table, and leaning his head on his hands, was engaged in silent prayer. Long they sat thus,—how long, they knew not. How terrible is that silent, speechless sorrow!

At length Mary rose, and throwing herself at her father's feet, she found relief in a flood of tears. "Oh, my dear father," said she, "believe me truthful. I am not to blame. Oh, speak to me! Let me hear you tell me again that you believe me innocent."

Her father raised her fondly, and fixing his eyes on her open, truthful face, he said, "Yes, my child; I do believe you innocent. It is impossible that crime could assume that look of candor and truth."

"But, my dear father," said Mary, "what will be the end of all this? What will become of us? Oh, if this danger threatened me only, I could bear it better. But I cannot bear that you should suffer on my account."

"Trust in God, my dear Mary," said James, "and do not fear. The very hairs of our heads are all numbered. Nothing can happen to us without the permission of God. Therefore nothing can happen that will not work for our good, and what more can we desire? Do not then be terrified; however you may be questioned, tell boldly the whole truth, and exactly the truth. Whatever they may promise, however they may threaten you, do not deviate a hairbreadth from the truth; keep your conscience clear: a conscience at ease is a pillow on which we may sleep soundly, even in a dungeon. They will probably separate us, my child. Your father will not be permitted to be with you in your sorrow. Cling, therefore, all the closer to your Father who is in Heaven, from whom they cannot separate you. Remember that no human power can separate us from the love of Christ."

James had scarcely finished speaking when the officers of justice entered. Mary uttered a piercing cry, and clung to her father.

"Separate them!" said the principal officer, in an angry tone; "bind the girl's hands and take her to prison: the father must also be confined for the present in some place whence he may be forthcoming when he is wanted. Let a guard be placed on the house and garden, and let no one enter without my permission. All the premises must be strictly searched."

His orders were obeyed. Poor Mary was torn from her father's arms, and her hands were tied. She fainted, and they carried her off, unconscious of what they did, while her father was led after, strictly guarded.

As they passed in this way through the streets of the village, crowds gathered to look at them, and many were the remarks that were made on all sides on their conduct. Good and charitable as James and Mary had been, they still had enemies who rejoiced in their fall. Mary, though gentle and amiable to all, had never mingled much with her neighbors in the village. Busy among her flowers, with a taste refined by her father's instructions, she disliked the coarse and silly gossip of the village women, who in their turn hated her for a superiority to them which they could not help feeling, even while they would not acknowledge it.

"So this is the end of Miss Mary's pride and fine airs!" said one of these evil speakers; "her father and she always seemed to think themselves better than anyone else. I always wondered how he could afford to buy all these fine flowers that she presented to the young Countess. No one but the young Countess was good enough for her, forsooth! But if this is the way they could afford to buy these rare flower roots, and make all these fine presents, I do not see that they have much to boast of."

All the inhabitants of Eichbourg, however, were not of this spirit. Some there were who had truly esteemed James, and who felt real pity for him and his daughter. Yet they, too, were now disposed to believe them guilty, so natural is it to the wicked human heart to believe evil rather than good of others.

"Poor human nature!" said some of these people, "who can one be sure of?" One would never have thought James and Mary would be guilty of such a thing."

"Who knows," said another, more disposed to think the best, "whether they have not been unjustly accused. If so, may God make their innocence manifest. And if they are guilty, may God grant them repentance, and support them under what they have to suffer. May God keep us from sin by his grace, for without his restraining grace we too might have fallen in the same way."

The children of the village mourned truly. They all loved Mary. Some of them were gathered in little groups, weeping as she passed. "It is wicked to put good James and Mary into prison," said they; "they are good people, they cannot have done anything wicked. Who will give us fruit and flowers now, and talk to us so pleasantly as Mary did?

Many voices were raised to attest Mary's goodness—many had received little kindnesses from her. The children were all agreed on the subject. "The officers were bad, naughty men," they decided, "who had no right to take good James and Mary to prison."

And this was all! Kind and blameless as their lives had been, not one honest voice was raised in remonstrance against the injustice—not one bystander in all that crowd was bold enough to step forward to say a friendly word of encouragement and comfort!

Such is the way of the world, so little is human approbation to be valued or depended on—so quickly does even unjust suspicion blight the character. There is but one Friend for the unfortunate who is unjustly accused, and that is," the Friend who sticketh closer than a brother."

Chapter Four

THROWN INTO A COLD PRISON CELL

MARY was carried still half unconscious into prison, and laid on the miserable straw which was to be her bed. Here she came to herself by degrees, and as she awoke to the full sense of her misery, to find herself alone in a prison cell, she wept and sobbed as if her heart would break, till, fairly exhausted by the violence of her agony, she sobbed herself to sleep on the wretched pile of straw, and slept for some hours. When she awoke, it was quite dark and cold and she did not at first remember where she was. All that had passed seemed like a frightful dream, till she was roused by feeling the fetters on her wrists. She started up at the horrible remembrance of her bonds, and kneeling on the floor of her cell, she prayed earnestly to God.—"Oh my God!" said she, "to whom can I go? From whom can I hope for help but from Thee? Thou canst hear me from my prison cell—Thou canst see me, when thus left alone by all. Oh God of all goodness, have mercy on me! Have mercy on my poor old father! Oh, holy and merciful Saviour, have compassion on me, and make my innocence manifest to all! Comfort my poor father, Oh Lord! and deliver him out of this trouble. Oh, have mercy on him, and save him; and if one must suffer, let it be me alone."

At the thought of her father, poor Mary's tears flowed afresh, sobs choked her voice, and she wept until it seemed that she could weep no more. At length a light appeared in the darkness of her prison cell. The moon rose, and its soft rays shone through the little grated window, and traced a shadow of the grating on the floor of the cell. By this soft light Mary was able to see the four walls of her cold, narrow prison, the coarse bricks of which it was built, the stone table in one corner, the little earthen plate and pitcher of water placed upon it, and the couch of straw on which she had been lying. Sad as this sight was, the gleam of light had comforted Mary, she had been so oppressed by the darkness and solitude.

The moon seemed like a well-known friend, and she rejoiced to see its soft beams shining on the floor of her lonely cell. She thought of the pleasant evenings when she had lain awake in her own little room in her dear cottage home, watching the same lovely light as it played through the branches of the rose bush that hung round her window, and traced their light foliage in shadow on the white curtains of her little bed. How gay the moonbeams seemed to her then, as they played through the flowers, gently waving in the wind! But now, through that still grating, they looked cold and sad. Still the light was pleasant, and as she gazed at it, she wondered if her father were gazing at it too—if the same beams were shining on them both.

While watching the moonlight, Mary thought she felt the perfume of flowers in her cell. She found it came from a little nosegay which she had tied up and fastened in her dress when she went to the castle in the morning. These flowers still retained their sweetness, and perfumed the air of the cell. She untied the flowers, and looked at them one by one in the light of the moon. "Oh," thought she, "when I was so happy this morning gathering these rosebuds in my garden and these forget-me-nots in the little brook, who could have believed that in the evening I would be in prison; when I wove the wreath of roses, and tied it round the basket, who could have thought that fetters would be on my hands before night. Nothing is certain—nothing abiding in this world. No one knows how quickly his fate may be changed; and no one can foretell that even his innocent actions may not end in misery. How needful it is, then, every day to implore the blessing of God, who alone can preserve us from all the unseen changes which we cannot avoid by any foresight of our own, and who can strengthen and guard us through them."

Mary wept again as she thought on the sad change that had come over her once happy life; her tears fell upon the flowers, and glittered like dew-drops in the moonbeams. She thought of the refreshing dew, and she said to herself, "He who does not forget the flowers, and who sends them refreshing rain when they are thirsty, will not forget me. Oh my God, I pray thee send comfort into the heart of my poor father and into mine, as thou sendest the dew-drops into the hearts of the thirsty flowers. How well these flowers remind me of my poor father's lessons," continued Mary to herself; "what a comfort to remember them now. These rosebuds have grown in the midst of thorns; thus do I hope that for me joy will spring up in the midst of suffering. If I had tried to open this rosebud, and to take it from its green covering before its time, I would have spoiled it. Slowly, one by one, the lovely leaves unfold, shedding around their rich perfume. Thus may I hope that God will remove my affliction in his own good time, and will make it produce blessings for me. I will try to wait patiently for him. These forget-me-nots make me think of Him who made them so beautiful. Oh my God, enable me always to remember thee, and do thou remember me. These little flowers are blue as the heavens above. The hope of heaven will support and console me in my troubles. Here are some delicate sweet peas, with their white and rose-colored blossoms. The tender stems of this lovely flower would fall to the ground but for the support to which they cling. Thus, oh my God, may I cling to thee, and do thou enable me to rise above this earth and all its miseries. But it is this sweet mignonette* which more than all the others is diffusing this perfume in my prison. Gentle flower! Thou refreshest even her whose hand plucked thee from the garden, and brought thee to this cold and dismal cell. I will try to resemble thee. I will forgive and pray for those who tore me from my happy home, and cast me into prison. Here is a fresh green sprig of periwinkle. It resists the winter's frost, and through all the cold season preserves its bright green color, the emblem of hope. God, who preserves this little flower green and fresh in the snow and ice, will also preserve me through the storms of misfortune. Here are some laurel leaves. They remind me of the immortal crown prepared in heaven for those who suffer patiently on earth—those who suffer with their Master; to whom he has promised that they shall also reign with him. I can imagine I see this splendid crown of glory, this unfading wreath. Flowers of earth! you are fading like its joys—you wither and die in an hour. But after the fleeting troubles of this life are over, we look for a glory and a happiness that can never fade away."

A dark cloud came over the moon. Mary could see her flowers no longer. The cell became frightfully dark for some time, but the cloud soon passed by, and the moon appeared again in all its beauty. "Thus," thought Mary, may innocence be obscured for a moment, but sooner or later it will shine forth again. The dark clouds of suspicion have gathered thickly round me, but God will yet dissipate them all, and make my innocence of this crime clear as the noonday."

Mary knelt in her cell, and prayed earnestly to God. She then lay down on her couch of straw, and repeated to herself some of the many passages of the Bible which were engraven on her memory. Thus occupied, she fell asleep as peacefully as if she were in her own little room. As she slept she dreamed a pleasant dream.

---

* Mignonette is a herbaceous plant with spikes of small fragrant greenish flowers.

She thought that she was walking by moonlight in a garden she had never seen before. This garden was of surpassing beauty, such as is only seen in dreams, and it appeared to be planted in a lonely desert, and surrounded by dark fir trees. The moon seemed brighter than it ever does in waking reality. All at once she saw her father in this enchanting place. He was smiling and happy. Mary rushed in fancy to meet him, threw herself into his arms, and shed tears of joy, which still moistened her cheek when she awoke. It was but a dream, yet she felt comforted.

Chapter Five

MARY'S TRIAL

MARY was barely awakened, when an officer came to conduct her before the tribunal. A cold shudder came over her as she entered the gloomy vaulted room, where the light of day could scarcely penetrate through the small panes of the high Gothic windows. The judge was sitting on a raised seat covered with scarlet, and the clerk was below, near a large old desk blackened by time. The judge asked Mary many questions. She answered them all truthfully; and she declared her innocence, even with tears. But the judge said coldly, "You cannot deceive me so far as to persuade me of that which is impossible. No one but you had been in the room; you must have the ring; confess it at once. Mary answered weeping, "I can say no more than I have already said. I have not the ring. I have not even seen it."

"The ring has been seen in your hand," continued the judge; "how will you answer that?" Mary said that this was impossible; and the judge ordered Margaret to be summoned.

To account for her appearance, it is necessary to relate what had passed at the castle in the meantime. On the day that the ring was missed, Margaret, still angry at the loss of the dress, to which she imagined herself entitled, and jealous of Mary, thought it a good opportunity to be revenged. She said openly to the servants in the castle, "This wretched flower-girl must have taken the ring. I met her as she was leaving the castle, and I saw a ring in her hand set with jewels; she was looking at it, but when she saw me, she hastily put it out of sight. It looked suspicious, but I thought it best to say nothing. She is such a favorite, I thought the Countess might have given it to her, as she has given her so many things before, and I determined not to speak rashly. I am very glad I did not happen to go into the Countess's room at the time. Such wicked hypocrites as Mary may cause honest people to be suspected.

Margaret's words were repeated, and she was consequently summoned as a witness on the trial. When she appeared before the tribunal, and the judge admonished her to speak the truth, her heart beat violently, and her knees trembled; but this wicked woman resisted the voice of conscience and the warning of the judge. "If I confess that I have told a lie," thought she, "I shall be dismissed from the castle in disgrace." This fear hardened her heart; and she even dared to say to Mary, "You have the ring; I saw it in your hand."

Mary shuddered with horror when she heard this calumny, but she bore it patiently; she only said, "You know, Margaret, that this is not true; you did not see the ring in my hand; how can you thus perjure yourself in order to injure one who has never done you any harm." But Margaret, influenced both by the fear of disgrace and the love of revenge, persisted in her falsehood; and, after being cross-questioned in vain, was dismissed.

"Your guilt is now evident," said the judge to Mary; "every circumstance is against you. The Countess's maid has seen the ring in your hand. Now, confess where you have concealed it."

Mary persisted in saying that she had it not; and, according to the barbarous custom of these times, he ordered her to be whipped till the blood came, to compel her to confess. Poor Mary screamed and wept; but, steadfast to the truth, she continued to protest that she was innocent. Pale, bleeding, and exhausted, she was again thrust into her cell. She suffered cruelly from her wounds, tossing on her uneasy bed. But she remembered her father's parting words. He had said, "When I am separated from you, cling closer to that Saviour from whom no human power can separate you." She had recourse to prayer, and God, who hears and answers prayer, sent her a sweet and refreshing sleep.

The next day, Mary was brought again before the tribunal, and the judge, finding severity of no use, tried to induce her to confess by gentleness and by promises. "You have incurred the punishment of death," said he, "but if you will only confess where the ring is, you shall be set free. No further punishment shall be inflicted upon you." His promises had as little effect as his threats. Mary repeated her former words. The judge, observing her tender affection for her father, tried to work upon this feeling. "If you continue obstinate," said he, your father also shall be punished. Have pity on his gray hairs. Could you bear to see his head fall under the executioner's axe. He must have helped and encouraged you in crime; and he, too, must die, unless you will yet save him by a full confession. Mary's courage gave way when she heard these words: she nearly fainted. "Confess," said the judge, "that you have taken the ring; that one word 'yes' may save your father's life."

This was a severe trial to Mary. She was long silent. She was tempted to say that she had taken the ring, and that she had lost it on the road, but she resisted the temptation. "No," said she at length, as if speaking to herself, "it is better to die than to sin. I cannot save my father's life, if it is only to be done by sinning against God. I will still trust thee, oh my God; thou wilt yet save us." She then continued, in a loud and firm tone, "If I were to say that I took the ring, it would be a lie, and I dare not tell a lie even to escape death. But oh," she added, in an agonized voice, "I implore you to be satisfied with taking my life. I would gladly die to save my father." The judge, notwithstanding his severity, was deeply moved. He said no more, and ordered Mary to be taken back to prison.

Chapter Six

A PAINFUL MEETING

THE judge was much embarrassed. "This is the third day that we have tried to discover the truth," said he to his clerk," and we have not advanced a single step. If I could see it to be possible that anyone else could have taken the ring, I would believe this young girl innocent. Such obstinacy at her age is incredible. But the evidence against her is too clear; she must have stolen it."

The judge went again to see the Countess, and questioned her closely. He examined. Margaret again; he spent the whole day in going over the minutes of the trial, and in considering the evidence with the utmost attention. At length, late in the evening, he ordered James to be brought into his study.

"James," said he, " you know that I have been thought severe, but you will do me the justice to say, that, though strict, I am not cruel or unjust. You know that I do not wish your daughter to suffer. Unfortunately the evidence against her is clear and indisputable, and by the law she deserves to die. The lady's-maid's evidence cannot be got over. Nevertheless, if she would confess and restore the ring, she might receive a pardon on account of her extreme youth; but, if she continue obstinate in her denial of the crime, there is no hope of saving her. Go then, James, and advise her; persuade her to restore the ring, and I pledge my word that no harm shall happen to her. You are her father; you have unbounded influence over her; if you do not make her confess, what can we think but that you are the accomplice of her crime? If the ring is not found, it will go hard with you."

"I will gladly see her and speak with her," said James; but I know that she has not stolen the ring, and that, consequently, she has nothing to confess. I will, however, converse with her; and if, innocent as she is, she must die, it will at least be a great consolation to me to see her once more."

The jailer conducted the old man to his daughter's cell; and having set down a lamp on the stone table, he withdrew, locking the door as he went out.

On the table, beside the lamp, stood a pitcher of water and a morsel of coarse bread, intended for Mary's supper, but it was untouched. She was lying with her face turned to the wall, and appeared to have been sleeping. The sound of footsteps, and the glimmer of the lamp roused her. She turned, and saw her father; and starting up, she threw herself into his arms. They wept for some time in silence. At last James told her the commission he had received.

"Oh, my dear father," said Mary, "surely you do not doubt my word? Is it possible that there is no one, not even my good father, who believes me innocent. I implore you to believe me! Indeed—indeed—I am not a thief!"

"Be calm, my dear child," said her father.

"I do most firmly believe you. I did not doubt you for a moment. I was merely telling you, as I promised to do, the commission with which I was charged."

James saw, with extreme pain, the change that a few days of suffering had made upon Mary. Her cheeks were pale and hollow; her eyes red and swollen; and her hair had fallen in heavy and disordered masses over her face and neck.

"My poor child," said he, God has sent you a severe trial. You have suffered much already; and I fear—I much fear—that the worst is yet to come. Innocent as you are, they will not believe it. They may be permitted to carry their cruelty still further. You ought to be prepared for this, my poor child. Do you know that they have the power to take away your young life?"

"My dearest father," said Mary, "I have no fears for myself. I could bear all they could inflict, if it would save you. But you—my dear father—the judge threatened you. He told me they would kill you. Oh! I cannot bear even to think of it."

"Compose yourself, my dear Mary," said James. "Have no fear for me; the judge said this only to try you. I am in no danger; but with you it is different."

"Oh!" interrupted Mary, joyfully; "then my heart is relieved of a heavy burden. If you are safe, my dear father, all is well; I do not fear death. I hope to go to God my Saviour. I shall meet my dear mother in heaven. What happiness this will be!" These words pierced to the very heart of the poor old man, and he wept like a child.

"God be praised," said he, as soon as he could speak, "God be praised for the happy state of mind in which I find you, my darling Mary. But it is cruel—very cruel—for an old father thus to lose his beloved child his only comfort, his last earthly treasure, the crown and joy of his old age! But, Oh Lord, thy will be done," continued he, in a faltering voice. "Thou demandest a great sacrifice, but I give it cheerfully. If it please Thee to take my daughter, I am resigned to Thy will; Thou knowest what is best. And oh, dear Mary, better lose you thus, than see you spared and led astray from what is right. Better you should die innocent—better be early removed from this cold world to heaven, than be spared for, perhaps, severer sufferings. May God strengthen you, my child. May He enable you to feel that His will is best."

A torrent of tears interrupted his words. After a pause, he added, "There is one thing more, dear Mary. Margaret has witnessed falsely against you. If you are condemned, it will be on her testimony—she will be the cause of your death. But you pardon her, do you not, my child? You are free from any feeling of hatred to her? Ah! you are happier than she is, though you are lying on this straw in this gloomy cell, and she is living in comfort and luxury in the castle. It is better to die innocent than to live with a guilty conscience. Forgive her, my dear Mary, as your Saviour forgave his murderers. You have done so have you not?"

Mary answered, "Yes, my dear father, I forgive her, and I pity her. She must feel very miserable when she thinks of what she has done. May God give her repentance and change her heart."

At that moment they heard the jailer's step in the passage.

"I must leave you, my beloved child," said James, "I commend you to God and to your Saviour. Trust in Him, dear Mary; He will strengthen you. And if I am never permitted to see you again, my darling—if this is the last time we are ever to meet on earth—we shall soon meet in heaven, for I feel that I cannot long survive you."

The jailer warned James that it was time to go; but Mary still held him fast— she could not part with him. He gently disengaged himself from her arms, kissed her for the last time, and turning quickly away, she fell fainting back on her straw.

James was conducted again to the presence of the judge. There he raised his hand to heaven, and, in a solemn voice, he said, "I believe my daughter innocent; I am ready to confirm it upon oath."

"I could almost believe it too," said the judge; but, unfortunately, my decision must be given, not according to what you and your daughter say, but according to the evidence in the case, and the strict letter of the law."

Chapter Seven

SENTENCED

EVERY one in the castle, and in the village, was exceedingly anxious to know what sentence would be pronounced on Mary. They trembled for her life; for in these times theft was punished with excessive severity. Many had suffered death for stealing articles of much less value than the ring. The Count earnestly desired that Mary's innocence could be proved. He carefully re-examined all the evidence he had many a consultation with the judge; but they could discover no means of acquitting her, for it seemed an utter impossibility that anyone else could have taken the ring. The Countess and her daughter earnestly entreated for Mary's pardon, and even implored it with tears. Poor old James, unable to help her in any other way, spent his time in almost incessant prayer for her. Every time that Mary heard the jailer's step, she imagined that he was coming to lead her to execution. The people in the prison had, in truth, begun to prepare for it. One day, as Margaret was passing, she saw some of these preparations, and she was struck with remorse.

That evening all the servants in the castle perceived that she was suffering some concealed agony of mind. She passed a wretched night. Mary's pale face haunted even her dreams; yet this miserable creature had not the courage to do what she could to atone for her crime, by confessing it in time to save Mary.

The judge at length pronounced sentence. Although Mary had incurred the punishment of death, it was commuted into a sentence of perpetual banishment, in consideration of her youth, and of her previous excellent conduct. This sentence was extended to James also; and everything they possessed was confiscated, as it was taken for granted that he was either the accomplice of her crime, or that his bad example or neglect had helped to lead her astray. Her punishment would have been more severe had it not been for the earnest entreaty of the Count and his family. James and Mary were ordered to be conducted over the border by the police; and their journey was to begin the very next day.

Early in the morning, as Mary and her father passed before the castle-gate with the police officer, Margaret came out. She had recovered her usual spirits. She did not wish that Mary should be put to death, but she had no objection to her banishment. As soon as she found that Mary's life was spared, her jealousy of her revived in full vigor. She hated her still, and still envied her the love that the young Countess had shown her. A few days before, Amelia having seen on a sideboard the basket which Mary had given her, had said to Margaret, "Take this basket out of my sight; it recalls so much that is painful, that I cannot bear to see it." Margaret took the basket and kept it in her own room, and now brought it out at this trying moment. "Here," said she, "take your fine present, Miss Mary; my lady can receive no presents from such as you. You thought yourself high in her favor; but all your fancied greatness has withered, like the flowers you brought, for which you were so well paid. I have the greatest pleasure, Miss Mary, in giving you back your fine basket." So saying, she threw the basket at Mary's feet; and with a sneering laugh, she went back into the castle, shutting the gate, as she passed, with a loud noise.

Mary, with tears in her eyes, silently picked up the basket, and went on her melancholy way. Her poor father had nothing, not even a stick to support his tottering steps, and her basket was now her only possession.

With eyes blinded with tears, she passed each familiar spot. She gazed on the cottage where she had spent so many happy days; and turned to look again and again at this dear home, till first the cottage, then the castle, and last of all, the spire of the village church, disappeared, from her sight behind a hill covered with trees.

When Mary and James reached the frontier, in the middle of a deep forest, the police officer left them. Poor old James was by this time so worn out with grief and fatigue that he could walk no farther, and sank down exhausted on a stone covered with moss, under the shade of an old oak tree.

After resting for a few minutes, he called Mary to his side. "Come, my child," said he, making her kneel down by him; "before we leave our native country, let us give thanks to God who has saved you from death—who has restored you, my darling to me and who has given to us both freedom to go where we will, and to enjoy the fresh air under the open sky, instead of being immured in a close and gloomy prison."

Then raising his eyes to heaven, he prayed thus: "Our Father which art in heaven, the only hope of thy children upon earth, the Protector of the oppressed, we thank Thee that Thou hast saved us from fetters, from prison, and from death. We thank Thee for all the blessings Thou hast given us during our past life. We thank Thee for all the blessings Thou art still giving us, in sparing us to each other, and in giving us freedom from bondage—in bestowing on us the support of Thy word and Thy promises in this life, and the glorious hope of a blessed immortality beyond death and the grave, through our Lord Jesus Christ. We cannot leave our native land without imploring Thy merciful care and guidance in the foreign land to which we are driven. Deign, Oh Lord, to look down in pity on an afflicted old man and his suffering child, and take us under Thy merciful protection. Be our guide and guard through the dangers to which we may be exposed. Conduct our steps, we pray Thee, among those who are Thy people, and incline their hearts to pity us. Grant us, Oh Lord, in this Thy world, a little corner, where we may finish our pilgrimage in quiet, and die in peace. We believe that Thou hast already prepared for us our destined habitation, though we know not where it is. Enable us to go on our way in faith and trust in Thee, till Thou shalt bring us to the place where Thou choosest us to dwell. Strengthen us, we pray Thee, for our journey, and grant us Thy peace, for our Lord Jesus Christ's sake."

When they had thus prayed (for every word of her father's prayer was re-echoed in Mary's heart), they rose up from their knees refreshed and comforted, and prepared to go on their way with courage, and even with joy. So wonderfully does prayer relieve and strengthen the soul.

Prayer is the simplest form of speech
That infant lips can try;
Prayer 's the sublimest strains that reach
The Majesty on High.
Oh Thou, by whom we come to God—
The Life, the Truth, the Way,
The path of prayer Thyself hast trod—
Oh! teach us how to pray.

Chapter Eight

A FRIEND IN MISFORTUNE

JUST at the moment that James had ended his prayer, the sound of a footstep was heard among the withered leaves, and Anthony, the old forester, appeared, coming towards them through the trees. He was an old and dear friend, for he had been a Huntsman for the Count, and had traveled with him when James was also of the party. Thus they had spent many pleasant days together in distant lands, and their friendship had been uninterrupted since. Anthony now served as the Count's Forester, and had been out early that morning at his work in the woods.

"God bless you, James," said he, "I am thankful I am in time to see you. I thought I heard your voice through the trees. It is then true that they have had the cruelty to banish you. It is a hard thing for a man to be obliged to leave his fatherland and his home after he has come to our time of life."

"As far as the blue arch of heaven extends, the land belongs to my Father in heaven," said James," So I may find a fatherland anywhere. We cannot be banished from his presence, or sent where his goodness will not follow us, but our true home is in heaven."

"And can it be possible," said Anthony, indignantly, "that they have actually robbed you of everything, and sent you away without even the necessary clothing for your journey?"

"He who clothes the lilies of the field," replied James, "will also clothe us."

"But have you no money with you at all?" asked Anthony.

"We have the treasure of a good conscience," said James, "which is greater riches than gold or silver."

"Is this empty basket, then," said the forester, "literally all you have brought with you? What may it be worth? A crown, perhaps," continued he, looking at it.

"If it is worth that, we are rich," said James; "if God continues to me the use of my hands, and blesses my labor, I can easily make a hundred of these baskets in a year, and we can live well on a hundred crowns. My father was a basket-maker, and he taught me his trade, that I might have an occupation for my leisure hours in winter. He could not bear to see me sitting idle. I bless his memory for having taught me so early habits. of constant industry. It is better for me than if he had left me a large legacy, and had, at the same time, allowed me to learn idle habits. A good conscience, health of body, and a respectable trade, are the best fortune anyone need wish for on earth."

Well, I am glad to see you bear your misfortunes so well," said Anthony. "I must confess, too, that you are right. Your knowledge of gardening will be also a great help to you. But where are you going now to look for work?"

"We are going far away," said James, "to some place where we are not known. God will guide our steps."

"My friend," said the forester, "I cannot do much to help you, but will you take this thick knotted stick of mine. I am glad I thought of bringing it today to help me to climb the hill. You will need one for your weary journey; and here," said he, drawing out a little leather purse, "here is some money which I received last night in payment for some wood in the village down there, where I slept last night."

"I will be very glad to take the stick, and I thank you very heartily for it," said James, "but I cannot accept any money for it. If it is a payment for wood, it belongs to the Count."

"My good honest friend," said the forester, "do not be concerned on that score; the money has already been paid to the Count. I advanced it some time ago for a poor man who had lost his cow, and had not any money to pay for the wood which he had bought. He has prospered better since that time; and yesterday, when I did not at all expect it, he repaid me the loan with thanks. It has just come in time for you; take it as a gift which God sends to you."

"Well, I will take it, then, my kind generous friend," said James, "and may God reward you. See Mary," continued he, addressing his daughter, "how God is already blessing us on our way. Before we have taken a single step in a strange land, he has sent this good old friend to meet us with money for our journey. Scarcely had we risen from our knees when we began to receive an answer to our prayers. It is, in truth, a fulfillment of his own blessed promise, 'When they call, I will answer; and while they are yet speaking, I will hear.' Let us, then, trust and not be afraid. God will continue to watch over us."

The old forester took leave of them with tears in his eyes. Good-bye, my honest friend James!—Good-bye, my good little Mary!" said he, shaking hands heartily with them both. "I know you are innocent. I have always known you to be worthy people, and I continue to believe it. Do not be cast down; you will see the old proverb fulfilled, Truth will out at last.' God will not forsake those who trust in him as you do. May He bless you and guide you." Saying these words, the old forester turned hastily away, and took the road that led to Eichbourg. James took his daughter by the hand, and walked away in a contrary direction, like Abraham, "not knowing whither he went."

[Reader, If you find yourself in a state of distress—perhaps feeling isolated, without support, or abandoned—it's important to remember that you are not alone. There are sources of strength and comfort available to you, even in the darkest times.

In moments of despair, it can be helpful to reflect on timeless words of encouragement. Consider the sentiment expressed in the Psalms: "Why art thou cast down, Oh my soul, and why art thou disquieted within me? Hope thou in God, for I shall yet praise him who is the health of my countenance and my God." This passage encourages you to put your hope in God and his higher purposes. In doing so you will yet find reasons to be grateful.

These words remind us that even amidst hardship, there is potential for renewal and hope. By focusing on inner strength and the possibility of better days ahead, you may find the resilience to overcome current challenges.

Remember, difficult times are often temporary. Seek support from trusted sources, whether they be friends, family, your pastor, or spiritual practices that resonate with you. Your well-being and peace of mind are valuable, and there are always paths forward, even when they're not immediately apparent.]

Chapter Nine

THE WANDERERS FIND A HOME

MARY and her father wandered on for many days without finding either work or a place where they could settle. They had traveled more than twenty miles; the money Anthony had given them was nearly spent, although they had lived as frugally as they could. The very thought of asking charity was painful to them, yet at last they were compelled to do it, and painful indeed they found it. More than one door was rudely closed against them; sometimes a little morsel of broken bread was given with a careless or surly word of reproach, which they bore with meekness, and were contented with the dry bread and water from the nearest brook. Sometimes people, more charitably disposed, invited them into their cottages, and gave them a little soup or vegetables, or even such morsels of meat as were left from their own repasts. Often for many days together the poor wanderers had not one warm meal, and they were thankful to be allowed to spend the night in a barn.

One day their journey had been longer and more fatiguing than usual. They had taken a rugged and hilly path, and for a long time they had seen no house where they could ask refreshment. Worn out with fatigue and hunger, the poor old man was taken suddenly ill, and sank down pale and speechless on a heap of dried leaves. Mary was in an agony of terror. She sought in vain for water—not a drop was to be found near. She called aloud for help, but no voice replied. She hastily climbed the nearest height, and looked eagerly round to see if there were any cottage in sight where she could hope to procure assistance, and at length she saw, in the middle of the wood, on the opposite side of the hill, a solitary farmhouse, surrounded with beautiful meadows and fields of ripe corn. She ran down the hill as fast as she could, and reached the farmhouse quite breathless. With tears in her eyes and a faltering voice, she implored help for her father. The farmer and his wife, both elderly people, were charitable and kindhearted. They were touched by the tears and entreaties, the paleness and the terror of the poor girl. The farmer's wife said to her husband, "Harness a horse into the cart as soon as you can, we must bring this poor old man here."

The farmer hastened to get ready a cart. His wife threw into it cushions and blankets, and filled a little pitcher with water, and a small bottle with vinegar. Mary having heard that the cart road, which led round the foot of the hill, was much longer than the way by which she had come right across it, took the pitcher of water, and the vinegar, and hastened to return by the way which she came, that she might be sooner with her father. By the time that she reached him, he had recovered a little, he had raised himself up, and was looking eagerly round for Mary. His joy was great when she appeared bringing the water. The cart came soon after, and he was taken to the farm. Behind the farmhouse there was a small cottage attached to it, intended for the farm laborers. It happened then to be unoccupied, and here James was conveyed. The kind farmer's wife had prepared a good bed for him, into which he was put. She spared no pains to get everything comfortably arranged for Mary, and brought her everything she could think of to do the old man good. His illness was the effect of fatigue and want of food, and all he required was rest and nourishment. The good woman brought him plenty of milk, butter, eggs, and meal; she even sacrificed some of her favorite fowls to make him nourishing soup, and the young pigeons which she had been keeping to carry to market, were roasted for him when he was able to eat them. The farmer and his wife had been accustomed to go once a year to a large fair in the neighborhood, which they considered a kind of festival. They resolved this year to remain at home, and to spend the money, which they had laid aside for some little luxuries at the fair, in buying some wine and medicine to restore strength to the invalid. Mary could not find words to thank them, but when every day she gave thanks and praise to God, who had raised up these kind friends for them in their utmost need, she prayed most earnestly, at the same time, that God would bless and reward their benefactors, and restore to them a thousandfold all they were bestowing so freely.

Mary never left her father's side, yet she was not idle. Every moment she could spare from attending to his wants, she spent in sewing and knitting for the farmer's wife; her busy fingers never rested, and never seemed to tire. The farmer's wife was delighted with her activity and usefulness, her gentle and obliging disposition. As soon as James's strength was a little restored by good food and rest, he too was anxious to be busy. His first work was a beautiful basket for the farmer's wife. He had guessed her taste exactly. The basket was large and strong, but, at the same time, very pretty. He had dyed some willows red, and woven with them, on the cover of the basket, the initials of her name, and the date when it was worked. Upon the sides he had contrived to weave with willows, of various colors, a neat little picture of a cottage, with a few pine trees surrounding it. This gave great pleasure to the farmer's wife, who was flattered and pleased by the allusion to the name of the farm, which was called Pine Farm.

When James had quite recovered his strength, he said, one day, to the farmer and his wife, "I have been long enough a burden to you; I must now go and try to find work." The farmer taking him kindly by the hand, said, "What whim is this, my dear James. I hope we have not offended you in any way.

Why do you wish to leave us? It is not what I expected from a sensible man like you."

A tear came into the eye of the farmer's wife at the thought of losing them, for Mary was like a daughter to her. Stay with us, my dear friends," said she, "the season is far advanced, the leaves are yellow already, they will soon fall, winter is at hand. Do you really wish to make yourselves ill again?"

James assured them that his only reason for wishing to go was the fear of being troublesome and a burden to them.

"Troublesome to us!" replied the farmer, "how can that be? You have your own little cottage there, which was empty before you came; you are not at all in our way, and you work for more than we give you."

"Oh yes," said his wife, "Mary's knitting and sewing, alone, is far more than all you have cost us. And if you are able to get on with your basket-making, James, you will make money. The last time I went to the mill, in the village, I took your beautiful basket with me. Everybody coveted it, everybody wished to have one like it. I can get you as many orders as you please. You may sell as many as you can make, so if work is all that you want, just consent to remain with us."

James and Mary gladly agreed to stay, to the great delight of the farmer and his wife.

[Reader, Consider your personal value and contributions to society. If you were to find yourself in an unfamiliar environment, surrounded by strangers, would they observe godly qualities that would make your presence a blessing?

Reflect on your talents and how you apply them. Are you living a life that positively impacts others? Or have you perhaps become overly focused on your own needs and desires?

It's worth contemplating whether your absence would be felt. Have you cultivated relationships and made contributions that would be missed if you were no longer present? Are there people who rely on you or benefit from your actions?

These questions are not meant to induce guilt, but rather to encourage self-reflection. They can serve as a catalyst for personal growth and a more purposeful approach to life. Consider how you might develop skills, nurture relationships, or engage in activities that enhance your positive impact on the world around you.

Remember, every individual has the potential to make meaningful contributions, no matter how small they may seem. The goal is to glorify God and enjoy him always; in so doing you will be a good friend to others and the kind of person that others enjoy and benefit from your company.]

Chapter Ten

MORE LESSONS FROM NATURE

JAMES and Mary now considered themselves at home in their little cottage, and settled themselves there to work busily. They got it made comfortable, with a few indispensable articles of furniture, and they refused any longer to receive from the good farmer and his wife anything except what they really earned and paid for. Mary was delighted to have once more the feeling of home, and tried to make their small dwelling as like their dear old home as possible. While James worked at his baskets, she was busy with her needle, and their time passed pleasantly. They often spent their evenings with the good farmer and his wife, who were always glad to see them. In the long winter evenings, all the people employed on the farm sometimes collected round the farmer's pleasant fireside, and listened with eager delight to James's amusing stories, and improving conversation. These winter evenings were long remembered with pleasure by many of the party.

Near the farm, there was a large garden and orchard, which had been much neglected. The good farmer and his wife did not understand these matters, they were too busy with the necessary labor in their fields. James undertook the care of them. In Autumn he prepared the ground, and in the first days of spring, as soon as the snow disappeared, he and Mary were busy from morning to night. He laid out the garden anew, the walks were once more bordered with box, and the beds were divided in regular order, and separated by well graveled walks. From the neighboring town they managed to procure seeds and roots, such as they had had in the dear old garden at Eichbourg. The garden soon bloomed with a magnificence, and profusion of flowers, such as had never been seen before in this wild and secluded place—and it gave a bright and smiling aspect to the whole valley—while the orchard, pruned by James's skillful hand, blossomed so beautifully, as to promise a crop such as had never been seen in it before. The blessing of God was upon all that good old James undertook. As Pharoah's household prospered under Joseph's care, so all seemed to prosper when this child of God was the laborer. He rejoiced in seeing all thriving round him, and he seemed to feel that the old times had come back again. He was as busy as before in teaching his daughter the lessons inscribed on the flowers, not the same as before, for something new seemed to be sent to him with every new spring. There is no sameness in the voices of nature; they are ever varying, and ever new.

In the early spring, Mary wished to bring him her usual offering of early violets. She carefully searched the woods and hedges, and brought him her first bunch with a face beaming with joy.

"Well," said her father, "he who seeks finds;" but, added he, "it is worthy of notice, that the sweet violet is often to be found among thorns. Under thorn hedges you may often seek for it, and find it. There is a great teaching in this. There is no situation in life, so thorny and so miserable, that we may not find blessings under the thorns if we look carefully for them. Who could have believed, that after all our wanderings, we should find such rest and peace in this solitary cottage, in the middle of this lonely wood. Trust in God, dear Mary, and in every situation, however desolate it may seem at first, He will send you blessings hid among the thorns."

The wife of one of the neighboring villagers came one day to buy flax at the farm, and brought her little boy with her. While she was choosing the flax, and settling the price of it with the farmer's wife, the child escaped through the open door into the garden. Forgetful of the protecting thorns, he flew eagerly to seize the roses that were growing near the entrance. In his rude and eager grasp, the delicate flowers were torn and crushed, and his hands and arms were cruelly scratched by the thorns. His cries brought his mother and the farmer's wife to the garden, where they were soon followed by James and Mary, all alarmed by the unusual outcry. They found the child standing with bleeding hands, near the rose bush, trampling on the scattered rose leaves at his feet, and wishing that he had strength to destroy the bush which had hurt him so much.

"It is often so with children of larger growth," said James. "They grasp at forbidden pleasures, which fall to pieces and vanish in their hands, leaving sharp thorns and a cruel sting behind. Even lawful pleasures, if seized too eagerly, perish in our grasp; and we are then ready to blame anything, rather than our own too great impetuosity. God teaches us to be 'temperate in all things;' to use the world as not abusing it,' because the fashion of this world passeth away; remembering that there is no singular happiness here. Almost every pleasure has its attendant thorn. Only in the garden above shall we find the thornless rose."

One beautiful summer morning Mary called her father to look at her lilies in full bloom. The flowers were very beautiful, but as the garden had been long neglected, all Mary's care had not been able to subdue the weeds. The bad seed had been so long allowed to fall into the ground, that the thorns and thistles sprung up much faster than she was able to pluck them up. Her beautiful lilies were indeed lilies among thorns.

"Do you remember, my dear Mary," said James, "that the church is compared, in the Bible, to a 'lily among thorns.' (Canticles 2:2.) Christ himself is likened to a lily, because of his purity, as the lily is of a spotless white; and because of his humility, as the lily is often found growing in lowly and humble places. His church is like him, as it is made up of true believers, and they all, in humble measure, are made like their glorious Master. By Adam's fall, man lost the image of God in which he was originally made; but in Christ, the second Adam, men are renewed in "knowledge after the image of him that created them.' (Col. 3:10.) And having the image of God once more created in them, in the new birth, they become, in humble degree, like Christ. He is like a lily among thorns; so are his church and people, in some measure, pure in an ungodly world, rising upright like the straight stem of the lily through the crooked and twisted and disordered mass around them, tending ever upwards, and reflecting the rays on the Sun of Righteousness, as the flowers of the lily reflect the sun on their pure white blossoms. The bright lily has no kindred with the thorns. It is evidently a plant of a different kind altogether; and one day God will transplant his lily to bloom in the garden where thorns are unknown."

"All fine plants," continued James, "have a natural tendency to rise upwards, and to turn to the light. In this respect we should learn a lesson from them. The soul of man, formed to soar upwards, should not grovel on the earth, and should ever turn to the light, shed abundantly from the Sun of Righteousness, the light of life (John 1:4), life giving, and life preserving." (John 8:12.)

One day James was transplanting young plants into a bed prepared for them, while Mary, a little further on, was preparing for him by clearing the ground from weeds.

"This double work," said James, is an emblem of that which ought to be the daily work of our lives; striving to uproot from our minds the evil habits which are natural to them, and to implant the graces which are not natural. And as now our work would not prosper unless God sent the gracious influences of the sun, and the rain, and the dew to make the young plants flourish, so neither can heavenly graces flourish in the soul unless watered by the dew of God's grace, and cherished by the gracious influences of his Spirit."

James was digging a part of the garden which had been long neglected. It was hard, and trodden down, and unfit for sowing seeds, because there was no "deepness of earth." He dug it deep, broke the clods, and turned them up to the surface to be crumbled by the hard frost.

"Just in this way," said he to Mary, "does God work upon hardened souls. They must be deeply pierced by sufferings and by convictions of sin; they must be exposed to the frosts of adversity, to soften their natural hardness, and to prepare the soil to receive the good seed. If the seed is sown without this preparation on the hardened soil, it has no deepness in it, and it soon withers; but after this deep digging, this severe exposure, it is no longer hard, the good seed takes root, and, blessed by God, bears abundant fruit."

The orchard had been as much neglected as the garden, and the trees required a great deal of pruning. They had all gone to leaf, and James had to use the knife very freely. He cut off all the green leafy branches which never blossomed, and left only the shoots likely to be fruit-bearing.

"See," said he to Mary, "here is the illustration of the verse (John 15:2) Every branch in me that beareth not fruit he taketh away; and every branch in me that beareth fruit, he purgeth it, that it may bring forth more fruit.' When there are the green leafy branches of profession and abundance of leaves, but no fruit, then God uses the pruning-knife. He cuts away and cuts down, if need be, almost to the ground; and after this pruning, the soul chastened and improved, begins to bring forth acceptable fruit."

James and Mary spent three years very happily at the Pine Farm. In the autumn of the third year, James's strength began visibly to decline. As the season advanced, his weakness and illness increased. By the time that the summer-flowers had almost disappeared, and the white, yellow, and purple crysanthemums were almost the last ornament of the garden, James was feeling seriously ill. He struggled on, however, and strove to work as long as he could, but he felt his strength daily diminishing, and he tried to prepare poor Mary for the affliction that he saw she must have to endure. His remarks on the flowers now often led to the idea of death, and the season helped to give his lessons more and more this cast of thought. His words made Mary feel sad, she scarcely knew why.

One day, she was attempting to gather her last autumn-rose, but though she touched it very gently, it fell to pieces in her hand.

"Such is man," said James; "in spring, bright and vigorous; in autumn, frail and weak. Yet, in God's people, this is only true of their bodies, and that only in this world: they will one day be raised up to unfading youth and beauty in heaven.

About this time, James was one day busy in pulling the best apples from a tree which was bending to the ground with its load of beautiful fruit, although the leaves were withering. James said, sadly, "The autumn wind is whistling through the withered leaves of the tree, as it is playing through the scanty locks of my gray hair. I am in the autumn of life, dear Mary; and if you are spared, you will also be so at a future time. Strive, and labor, and pray, that when your autumn comes, you may be found bearing fruit as abundantly as this tree, fruit which may be acceptable to the great Husbandman."

When Mary was sowing seeds for the following spring, James said to her, "Thus will our bodies be one day sown in the earth; sown in corruption, to be raised in glory; sown in weakness, raised in power; sown a natural body, raised a spiritual body; sown alone a poor miserable grain, planted to die, yet springing again to life, renewed in beauty, a thousandfold brighter and better than before. The day may not be far distant, my child, when you shall see my body thus laid in earth; but grieve not, my dear Mary, weep not, death is but the gateway to heaven, the passage to endless life, the preparation for immortality. The Saviour has conquered death and the grave, and we may gladly unite in the triumphant words of the apostle,—'Oh Death, where is thy sting? Oh Grave! where is thy victory? Thanks be to God, which giveth us the victory through our Lord Jesus Christ.'" (1 Cor. 15:55-57.)

While Mary listened to her father, her heart was too full for words. A sad foreboding seized her mind. She felt that James was trying to prepare her for his own death—a glorious change for him, but an unspeakable loss to her a loss that seemed too great to be realized: she dared not suffer her mind to dwell upon it, for it would have unfitted her for her daily duties.

Chapter Eleven

JAMES'S ILLNESS

WINTER set in with uncommon severity; the ground was early covered with deep snow. James became seriously ill. Mary wished to send for the doctor from the nearest village, and the kind farmer went in a sledge on the top of the snow to fetch him. When the doctor had seen James, and prescribed for him, Mary followed him to the door, and anxiously inquired if he thought her father in danger. The doctor said that he did not think there was any immediate danger, but there was a great risk that the attack might end in consumption, and that in this case, at her father's age, there would be no hope of his recovery. Poor Mary was sadly overcome on hearing this; but remembering that her tears would grieve her father, she exerted all her self-command to restrain them, that she might not hurt him, and she re-entered his room with a composed and serene face. It requires more true and deep feeling to act in this way than to give way to useless tears and lamentations, which are often the mere outpouring of selfishness. Mary's love for her father was real, and overcame her love of self. Her affection was shown, not by useless tears, but by active exertions for his comfort. His food was carefully and regularly prepared, nicely cooked, and served to him in the most inviting way. His pillows were skilfully arranged to give him ease; she watched his every look, that she might anticipate his wishes. She often passed the night watching by his pillow; and many a weary hour her busy fingers worked, to gain enough money to procure for him the little comforts that he needed. When she did lie down to rest, her sleep was often disturbed. If he coughed, or if he moved, she glided gently in to see if anything was wanting. When he was able to hear her, she read aloud to him: but, above all, her prayers were constant for him. Often when he was sleeping she was praying by his side, and weeping silently when he could not see her tears. She found relief in pouring out the distress of her soul before God. "Oh Lord, spare my father; spare him to me, I pray thee, even a little longer," was often her agonized cry; yet still she added, as she had been ever taught to do, "Thy will be done."

The old man recovered a little, but it was evident that the amendment was only temporary. He himself felt that death was approaching. He was calm and resigned. He spoke of it to Mary with the greatest composure. He wished to prepare her for the blow. Poor Mary could scarcely bear this. Notwithstanding her strongest efforts to control herself, her composure nearly gave way.

"Oh, my dear father," said she, "do not speak to me of losing you. The very thought is agony. I cannot bear it. What would become of me? I have no other friend on earth. I should be desolate indeed."

"Do not grieve so, my dear child," said her father; "Christians must not sorrow as those that have no hope. For me, death is a glorious change; and as to you, my darling, I can trust you with Him who has promised to be a Father to the fatherless. He has said, 'Leave thy fatherless children, and I will preserve them alive.' If your earthly father is taken away, dear Mary, you have your Father in heaven still. I have no anxiety about your worldly provision. He who feedeth the young ravens when they cry, will provide your food. He who clothes the grass of the field will much more clothe you. He has said, 'The young lions do lack and suffer hunger, but they that seek the Lord shall not want any good thing.' (Ps 34:10.) He has also said, 'Take no thought, saying, What shall we eat? or what shall we drink? or wherewithal shall we be clothed? for your heavenly Father knoweth that ye have need of all these things. But seek ye first the kingdom of God and his righteousness, and all these things shall be added unto you.' (Matt 6:31–33.) But remember, dear Mary, this exhortation,

'Seek ye first.' Let it be your daily prayer, your daily endeavor, to seek first, above all things, that righteousness which is the one thing needful. Keep close to Christ, and then you will have nothing to fear. If you are walking with Christ, seeking him daily in prayer, leaning on his arm, trusting in his strength, feeding on his word, you will be kept safe even in the midst of enemies. You have been brought up in great retirement, my child; you have hitherto been shielded from many of the temptations to which those are exposed who come more in contact with the world; but when I am taken away you may be thrown more among others, you may be exposed to conflict with various enemies, both within and without. You know, dear Mary, that these enemies are threefold—Satan, the world, and our own evil natures. I know you will shrink from wicked people when you know them to be such; but Satan can sometimes appear even as an angel of light; and if you trust to your own wisdom and discernment, my poor girl, you will be often deceived. 'Trust in the Lord with all thine heart, and lean not unto thine own understanding. In all thy ways acknowledge Him, and He shall direct thy paths.' (Prov. 3:5,6.)

Look always unto Jesus. It is by the daily walk with Him, the daily seeking from Him wisdom and strength, that we can alone hope to be preserved from the snares of the wicked. Then, besides outward enemies, we have a whole host of treacherous enemies in our own hearts, ever threatening to betray us, and to turn us away from seeking Christ daily. Indolence and Sloth will whisper to you, perhaps, that if you are busy or tired, there is no great harm in omitting your daily prayer; and Presumption will add, that you are in no particular peril at that moment. Procrastination will say, that another time will do as well as your stated morning hour; and Self-Indulgence will plead for a little less strictness. Evil tempers, murmuring and wandering thoughts, will try to distract your attention during prayer, if you cannot be quite hindered from it. When you feel the risings of these evil things within, my child, flee to Jesus; tell Him of your difficulties of your temptations; ask for strength to fight the good fight the incessant warfare with inward as well as outward temptations. You know the weapons of this warfare, dear Mary, that they are not carnal, but spiritual. I have often spoken to you about the armor of the Christian soldier. (Eph. 6:10-18.) Clothed with the armor, and looking ever to Jesus for strength, you may go safely on your pilgrimage, fearing no enemies, and all things will work together for your good. Even seeming evils are overruled by God for the good of his people.

"I can now look back on my past life and on all the way by which the Lord my God has led me, and bless him for his goodness to me. Yes, I can praise him for much that was painful to me at the time. When our eyes are opened by God's grace, and we see things no longer as the dark world sees them, but when 'God, who commanded the light to shine out of darkness, hath shined in our hearts, to give the light of the knowledge of the glory of God in the face of Jesus Christ,' we begin to set a different value on all things. We see that prosperity is sometimes a curse, and adversity a blessing. We understand better what constitutes true happiness. You know, my child, that I speak from experience. I at one time tasted largely of what the world calls pleasure. When I traveled with the Count, I was allowed to share in a very large degree in all the amusements that the world covets. I enjoyed all the luxuries that worldly people desire. I know the worthlessness of all to give happiness. I have enjoyed much more real happiness in an hour of meditation and communion with God in our dear old garden. Believe me, my child, there is no true blessedness but in God. Oh! my dear Mary, pray and strive to obtain that pearl of great price, which is the only treasure worth seeking.

"You know, my child, that I have not been without trials, yet I can thank God now for them, and feel that they were sent in mercy and in great love; for whom the Lord loveth he chasteneth, and scourgeth every son whom he receiveth. When your mother died, I suffered very deeply. My soul seemed dried up within me. It was broken up and furrowed, as you have seen the earth in a time of drought; yet, after a time, God sent the abundant and refreshing dew of his consolations, and revived my thirsty soul, and I felt the benefit of the affliction; for, by this trial, he weaned me more from earthly things, and helped me to set my affections on things above.

"God ever does this, dear Mary. If we trace the workings of his providence we shall always find that he brings good out of evil. Do you remember the miserable day, when, faint with fatigue and hunger, I fell down by the wayside? From that day's suffering, many of the comforts of the last three years have sprung. It brought us acquainted with these kind people, who received and sheltered us.

"Our greatest grief was when you were accused of theft and thrust into prison. Yet even in this severe trial, dear Mary, I think I can already see God's purposes of mercy to you. The young Countess had distinguished you by her favor, and wished to have you much with her. She had even begun to excite and foster vanity in you by her gifts. Had this friendship continued, you would have been exposed to many temptations; and young as you were, you might have been led astray from what was right. Depend upon it, dear Mary, that in this case, the path of adversity, though painful, was the safest. God used these means to deepen and elevate your character, to purge and to strengthen your soul, and to teach you more simple reliance on his faithfulness. It is another example of the truth of the words of Scripture, 'That though no chastening for the present seemeth to be joyous, but grievous; nevertheless, afterward, it yieldeth the peaceable fruit of righteousness unto them which are exercised thereby.' (Heb. 12:11.)

"At some future time, when the affliction has done its full work, and when you may be safely trusted to withstand temptation, it may perhaps be the good pleasure of God to remove this affliction altogether, to make your innocence clear in the sight of all, and to restore you to the favor and friendship of the Countess. But if it should not be so, my child; if, on the contrary, even severer trials are awaiting you, do not be afraid. If the wounds inflicted on you are deep, remember that the knife is in the hand of a loving Father. Our Lord Jesus Christ is a wise and skillful Physician, who will not give one unnecessary pang, who wounds only to cure. In the darkest and most trying days, trust him—hope on—faint not. Remember the experience and exhortation of the Psalmist, "I had fainted, unless I had believed to see the goodness of the Lord in the land of the living. Wait on the Lord; be of good courage, and he shall strengthen thine heart: wait, I say, on the Lord." (Psalm 27:13,14.)

"Yes, dear Mary, even my death, the affliction you dread so much, which it pains you so much to think of, will be overruled for good to you, though you cannot see this at present. Try, my dear child, to reconcile yourself to the thought, try to hear me speak of it with resignation. There is nothing terrible in death to a Christian. It is only the removal from the garden below to the garden above. Let us go back once more to some of the lessons of our old garden at Eichbourg. Do you remember our seed-beds, where the young shoots that were one day to be magnificent trees, came up weak and crowded together in a narrow bed? How miserable they looked then, without a vestige of the beauty which they were afterwards to have. When they were left long in the seedbed, do you remember how feeble and sickly they looked from want of air and room? You used to urge me to transplant them. You would not be satisfied till you had seen them removed to a bed prepared for them, where, with fresh air, and light, and sunshine, they soon shot up into luxuriance and beauty. Here, my child, we are like these feeble and miserable plants, with scarcely the appearance of life, and no beauty; but when God transplants us into his glorious garden above, he will clothe us with a beauty of which we have no conception here. 'Eye hath not seen, nor ear heard, neither have entered into the heart of man the things which God hath prepared for them that love him.' (1 Cor. 2:9.) But one thing we know, that when he shall appear, we shall be like him, for we shall see him as he is' (1 John 3:2); that when Christ, who is our life, shall appear, we also shall appear with him in glory. And is not this the sum of all happiness? Oh! my dear Mary, do not grieve that the time is drawing near when I shall be removed, to be made perfectly blessed. I am going to my Saviour, do not wish to keep me here. Only keep close to him now, that we may meet again above. If you are truly united to Christ, if you are made one with him, then you will have a community of interests with him; a community of suffering, in bearing patiently the cross that he sends, as he patiently bore a far heavier cross for you; a community of work, in laboring in the service of God; and a community of glory, in being made a partaker of his heavenly inheritance. Oh! Dear Mary, if we are really Christ's, the sufferings of this present time are not worthy to be compared to the glory which shall be revealed in us. Our light afflictions, which are but for a moment, shall work out a far more exceeding and eternal weight of glory."

Such were the conversations of James and his daughter; such the advice and instruction which he gave her from time to time as he was able to speak. Every word sank deep into the heart of Mary, and was watered by her tears. It fell into a soil prepared to receive it, for it had been deeply plowed by sorrow.

When James spoke of his death, she was sometimes wholly unable to command herself. "I have given you much pain, my child," said James, "yet I cannot part from you without giving you advice and warning. What is sown in tears, often produces a harvest of joy."

> "Watcher, who wakest by the bed of pain,
> While the stars sweep on with their midnight train,
> Stifling the tear for thy loved one's sake,
> Holding thy breath, lest his sleep should break:
> In the loneliest hour there's a helper nigh—
> 'Jesus of Nazareth passeth by.'

> "Fading one, with the hectic streak
> In thy vein of fire and thy wasted cheek,
> Fearest thou the shade of the darkened vale?
> Look to the Guide, who can never fail:
> He hath trod it himself, he will hear thy sigh—
> 'Jesus of Nazareth passeth by.'"

Chapter Twelve

MARY'S GREAT LOSS

As soon as James's illness had appeared dire, Mary went straightway to Erlenbrünnen, to ask the minister of that place to come and see her father, as the Pine Farm was in the minister's parish. The minister, a pious and worthy man, had paid several visits to the infirmed man; they enjoyed many pleasant conversations together, and his visits and his prayers were a great consolation to Mary.

One afternoon, when he came, he found James much weaker. He remained a long time alone with him; and after he went away, James said to his daughter, "My dear Mary, I do not think I shall ever be able to be out at church again, and tomorrow I hope to receive the sacrament here, from the hands of our good minister."

Mary felt this deeply. It seemed as if her father had given up all hope of recovery; but she strove to command her feelings for his sake. James spoke little during the day, and seemed much engaged in silent prayer. Next day the good minister came, and a little congregation was formed in James's room. The farmer, his wife, and several of the workers were present. They seemed all much moved and solemnized by the service, and Mary felt comforted and strengthened by it.

Notwithstanding all Mary's care, the old man continued to get weaker every day. The farmer and his wife, who loved him much, did all they could for him, and they often went to his room to inquire how he felt, or to help poor Mary in her anxious hours of watching. Mary often asked them, with a mixture of fear and hope, —"Oh, do you not think it is possible that he may yet recover?" —and they as often evaded answering her question. At length, thinking it cruel to deceive her, the farmer's wife said, in answer to her oft-repeated question, "My dear Mary, while there is life there is hope; but I do not think that your father will ever see the trees in leaf again, or the summer flowers in blossom."

From that moment, poor Mary dreaded the approach of spring. Till then she had welcomed it with joy; she had watched the first opening bud, the first green shoot appearing through the ground. But this year she dreaded to see it. The bright green hue, beginning to steal over the dry, brown branches, as the tiny buds began to expand; the snow-drop, raising its snowy head; the joyous song of the birds filled her soul with sadness. These signs of spring now seemed like the announcement of her father's approaching death. One day she opened her window to breathe the fresh air for a moment. It was one of these bright spring mornings, when all nature seems to rejoice. For the first time, these voices were at painful variance with Mary's feelings. "Must all things rise to new life," said she, "except my poor father? He is fading away, when everything is reviving and rejoicing. All things speak of life, and hope, and joy, and is there no hope for him?"

But even while she was speaking, Mary's conscience smote her for her forgetfulness of her father's lessons. She breathed a fervent prayer to God for strength to bear whatever it might be his will to send, and calm and peace returned to her soul. "My father, too, will rise to new life," thought she, "though not in this world. He is now only laying aside an old worn-out garment, to be clothed in immortal robes. His 'hope is fixed as an anchor within the vail, sure and steadfast.' He is going to fall asleep in Jesus, to rise to new life and glory. His true life is just going to begin."

The old man delighted in hearing Mary read aloud. She read with feeling, and her voice was very sweet and clear. How necessary a qualification this is for the watcher by a sick-bed! and how few really possess it! How few read with that softly-modulated voice, these distinct, clear, but gentle tones, which soothe the weary ear, and charm away the sense of pain! This is an accomplishment which no woman should be without, for all must have to watch one day at the bed of sickness and death.

One night, Mary was sitting silently beside her father. She had put out her lamp, for the moon was shining brightly into the room, and she loved to watch its beams. Her father, who had had a short sleep, awoke, and called her to him. "My child," said the dying man, read to me once more our Lord's last prayer for his disciples. Mary lighted her candle, and read to him from John Chapter 17.

"Now, raise me a little, dear Mary," said James, "and bring me the Bible." Mary put the Bible into his hand, and brought the candle nearer him. "Listen, my child," he said, "to the last prayer I offer for you." With a trembling voice, and marking the passage in the Bible with his finger as he spoke, he prayed thus: "Oh, my Lord and Saviour, thou art calling me to leave this world, and I must leave my child alone in it. But let her not be alone: be thou with her. May I go to thee, to be with thee where thou art, Oh my Saviour! and do thou preserve my child. I do not ask thee to take her out of this world till thou seest it best: but, Oh, I beseech thee, do thou keep her from the evil that is in the world. Sanctify her, I pray thee, by thy truth—thy Word is truth. Thou gavest her, Oh Lord, to my care in this world, and I have tried, as far as I could, to devote her to thee. If we must part now, Oh grant that we may meet again before thy throne, to be with thee forever and ever, and to behold thy glory; for the sake of our Lord Jesus Christ. Amen."

With a throbbing heart and a faltering voice, Mary whispered "Amen."

"Yes, my child," continued James, "I trust that we shall meet again above, and see our Lord Jesus in his kingdom. In the mansions above, which he has prepared for his people, there will be no more grief, no more sorrow, no more painful separations. God will wipe away all tears from every eye. There shall be no more death, nor sorrow, nor crying, neither shall there be any more pain. There shall be no night there, for the glory of God shall lighten it, and the Lamb shall be the light thereof."

He fell back on his pillow exhausted; he could speak no more for some time, and Mary stood by his side in silence. The Bible was still grasped in his hand. It was one which he had bought with his first savings after he had come to the Pine Farm, and it had been his constant companion and his great comfort in his illness. After he had rested a few minutes, he revived a little, and said, "I thank you once more, my darling child, for all your care and kindness to me in my long illness. You have been truly a dutiful child, and God will bless you. I leave you to his care. Trust in him, dear Mary, and he will provide for you, though I have nothing to leave you but my blessing and this book. I know you will value both, my dear Mary, more than any worldly thing.

This Bible only cost a few pence, and yet it is a richer treasure than gold or silver. It is a better legacy than gold or jewels, for it is the Word of God, and by it we learn to know that heavenly wisdom which is better than rubies. (Prov.iii. 13–18.) Take this Bible, my beloved child, as your father's last gift. Keep it as a remembrance of me. Read in it every day. However busy you may be, do not let any morning pass without reading at least a small portion of it. Try to fix a verse in your memory, to think of and meditate on through the day, when your hands are busy. If you do not understand any passage, pray to God to grant you his Holy Spirit to enlighten you. God himself, and he only, can open your eyes and make you see wonderful things out of his law; and if you pray to him, he will do this, and will give you day by day more knowledge of himself. Each verse, meditated on with prayer, will become a fresh treasure of heavenly wisdom. I have learned more from these few words, 'consider the lilies of the field,' than I learned in my youth from many a volume. These simple words have been the origin of my purest enjoyments; and in many an affliction, when I was ready to faint under the weight of the trial, they have revived my courage, strengthened my faith, and restored peace to my soul."

Again James was forced to cease speaking, from exhaustion, and he lay quiet till about three o'clock in the morning. He then said, faintly, "Open the window, Mary, I feel very ill."

She hastened to open the window. It was a clear night: the stars were shining bright. The fresh air revived the old man. "How brilliant the stars are!" said he; "What are the fading flowers of earth, when compared with the unfading glories of the sky! It is there I am going. Oh what joy! Come, Lord Jesus, come quickly!"

Saying these words, his head sunk back on the pillow, and he slipped away so quietly that Mary did not know it was death. She thought he had fainted; but when she drew nearer to try to revive him, she was seized with sudden fear. She had never seen that look before; that indescribable look, when once seen, never to be forgotten, of the mortal frame when the soul has just left it. She hastened to awaken the people of the house, and they told her her father was dead. The farmer's wife gently closed his eyes. Poor Mary could scarcely be persuaded to leave the bedside. She kissed his pale face; she implored them to leave her alone with him; she refused, almost frantically, to allow him to be moved or touched. At last she fainted, and while she was unconscious the kind farmer's wife carried her into her room, and laid her on her own bed, where she sat by her, gently soothing her, and weeping with her, while the other women quietly arranged her father's room. But thither Mary soon insisted on returning. She seemed unable to remain away from all that was now left to her of the father she had loved so much. The kind neighbors often persuaded her to come away for a little; but when they left her alone, she slipped quietly back to that cold, lonely room. She had been for months so accustomed to watch her father's slightest movements, that her straining ear, often deceived, imagined still to hear the well-known voice. Ever and again she would start, fancying she heard her father calling, her father moving, scarcely even now able to believe that she would never hear that much-loved voice again. Oh! who can describe the unspeakable anguish of the first days after a sore bereavement, when all is over, when the hope against hope that sustained to the last, through all the long weary hours of watching, is gone, and deprived at one stroke of all that has been the constant thought and care of every moment, the mourner is left bereaved and desolate indeed!

Mary's only comfort was in reading her father's Bible. With this well-worn book in her hand, she could almost fancy that he was still speaking to her. On the day that the coffin was going to be closed, Mary strewed in it some fresh spring-flowers, the first snowdrops and primroses, with some sprigs of rosemary.

Her father had loved flowers so much that she wished to put them near him, even at this last moment. These early flowers of spring were associated in her mind with all he had so often said to her of the resurrection of the body to a new and fresh life; and the rosemary, ever green and ever fragrant, she put in as an emblem of the unfading and pleasant remembrance which she would ever cherish of her kind and much-loved parent.

The funeral day was a sad trial to Mary, but she resolved to do her duty to the last. Dressed in deep mourning, she followed her father to the grave, calm and composed, but pale as death. Every one who saw her pitied the poor orphan, now left alone in the world. As James was a stranger at Erlenbrünnen, his grave was dug in a corner of the churchyard near the wall. Two large fir trees overshadowed the place. The minister addressed the people from these words, "Except a corn of wheat fall into the ground and die, it abideth alone; but if it die, it bringeth forth much fruit." (John 12:24.) He spoke first of the beauty and depth of meaning in this verse, as applied by our Saviour to his own death. He then considered it as applied to the death unto sin which must take place in each individual believer. Every soul united to Christ must die to self and sin before it can rise to new life in him. As the apostle explains it, "We are buried with him by baptism unto death, that like as Christ was raised up from the dead by the glory of the Father, even so we also should walk in newness of life. For if we have been planted together in the likeness of his death, we shall be also in the likeness of his resurrection." (Rom. 6:4, 5.) He spoke also of the twofold effect of this spiritual resurrection in this life. 1. That the power of sin is destroyed in believers. "Knowing this that our old man is crucified with him, that the body of sin may be destroyed, that henceforth we should not serve sin. For he that is dead is freed from sin." (Rom. 6:6, 7.) 2. That after this, being thus made free from sin, believers live to the glory of God. They have their fruit unto holiness. (Rom. 6:18-22.) They are no longer unprofitable, they bring forth much fruit. He then explained that it is only if we have been made partakers of this spiritual resurrection in this world, that we can have any sure hope of a resurrection unto life in the world to come.

As the life is never actually out of the seed, for though for a time it appears to die and decay, the principle of life remains hid, and this is quickened into new life and fresh vigor when it springs anew: so when the believer dies, and his body is laid in the grave, his life is hid with Christ in God; and when Christ, who is his life, shall appear, then shall he also appear with him in glory.

The minister concluded his address by speaking of the sure hope they might have of the resurrection unto life of the good old man who was that day laid in the grave, because he had been a true believer; one of those really united to Christ, as had been evident to all by his holy and consistent walk and conversation, and by his incessant labors for the spiritual good of others. He reminded those who had profited by his good counsels, to show their gratitude, by their kindness to his daughter. He spoke of the peculiar duty laid upon all who profess to be Christians, to visit especially the fatherless and widows in their affliction. (James 1:27.)

Mary often visited her father's grave to think of him, to recall to mind his cherished counsels, and to pray there for strength to follow them. She loved the perfect calm and tranquility of that lonely churchyard. It seemed that thus in the very presence of death, she felt more separated from earth, and more filled with earnest longing for the day when all that are in their graves shall hear His voice, and shall come forth. Thus meditating on the coming of the Lord, she staid her soul on Him, the only true comforter; and never did she feel more serene and resigned than after a visit to the churchyard.

Chapter Thirteen

MORE SORROW

WHEN all was over, and poor Mary began her everyday work again, she was often plunged in deep sadness. She had loved her needlework when she was enlivened by her father's interesting conversation, but it was dreary work to sew or knit alone, with no companion but her own sad musings. Her busy fingers had worked joyfully, when they were laboring for her father's comfort, but now all motive for exertion seemed taken away. She missed every day, more and more, his kind voice, his warm affection, his good counsels. Everything now looked gloomy; the dark firs in the wood round the farm appeared to be clothed in mourning. Perhaps it was well for Mary to be roused, and prevented from brooding over her grief, even although this was done by new trials which came upon her.

Great changes took place at the Pine Farm soon after her father's death. The son of the farmer, who had been for some time absent from home, had told his parents, shortly before, of his intention to marry; and when his marriage took place, the old father and mother, longing for quiet and freedom from care in the end of their days, gave up the farm to their son, on condition of his providing for and taking care of them in their old age. Their new daughter-in-law was rather pretty, and very rich, but she had no mental recommendation. She had two ruling passions, vanity of her beauty, and the love of money. Conceit and avarice reigning in her heart, had, of course, carved their lines upon her face, so that, notwithstanding her good features, she had a most disagreeable expression.

With such a woman at the head of the household, it may easily be believed that there was little comfort for anyone in the house. As she had no principle, and cared not for duty, she wholly disregarded her husband's father and mother. She seemed even to have a perverse pleasure in doing what they disliked; she provided nothing for their comfort, except what she was absolutely obliged to do, by the conditions on which her husband held the farm, and she seemed to grudge them every morsel. The good old couple retired into the cottage formerly occupied by James, and tried to keep out of their daughter-in-law's way as much as they could. This undutiful daughter was no better as a wife, for she who is undutiful in one relation of life, seldom fails to be equally bad in all. She made her husband's life perfectly miserable. She reminded him perpetually of the large fortune she had brought him, which, she seemed to think, entitled her to treat him as her slave. She was jealous of his love for his parents, and would hardly ever allow him to see them in peace. It was only when he could slip away unperceived, that he ventured to go and sit with them, and to relieve his mind by telling them of his troubles.

"My poor son," said the farmer, "we have all made a great mistake. You were foolishly caught by a pretty face; your mother was pleased with your intended bride's large fortune; and I, who ought to have known better, was foolish enough to yield to your united entreaties. Now we are all three punished for our folly. I wish I had taken good old James's advice on this subject. He never approved of this marriage. I well remember his words, for I have often thought of them since. Do you remember, wife, one day you said to him, 'Well! 10,000 florins is a good sum, something worth having.' 'Not at all worth having,' said James, unless there is something better along with it. A good wife is indeed a treasure, "her price is far above rubies" (Prov. 31:10), even if she has not a farthing of money. But unless your son marries a wife with the fear of God, her money will be only like a millstone round his neck, a burden, which it will be a torture to bear, and which may even make him despicable in his own eyes. Why do you care so much for money? It is not a thing to be so greatly desired. Remember Agur's prayer, "Remove far from me vanity and lies; give me neither poverty nor riches; feed me with food convenient for me." (Prov. 30:8.) There is great wisdom in this prayer. Remember also the saying of Timothy, "They that will be rich, fall into temptation and a snare, and into many foolish and hurtful lusts, which drown men in destruction and perdition. For the love of money is the root of all evil." (1 Tim. 6:9,10). These were James's very words, I think I hear him still. You, my son, said to him one day. 'But you must confess that she is a beautiful creature, as bright and fresh as a rose.' And James replied, 'A rose is not merely beautiful, it is also fragrant and useful. From real flowers we get many useful things, honey, and wax, and perfume, and many more besides. But beauty, without piety, is like an artificial rose, a rose made of paper, a miserable imitation which has no other good quality. It pleases the eye at a distance, but grievously disappoints us on a nearer view, and is absolutely useless.' Thus honest James warned us, but we did not listen to his advice, and we must now bear the consequences as well as we can. Since our misfortune is irrevocable, let us pray to God for patience, and bear it meekly."

Such were the conversations that passed between the farmer and his son.

Poor Mary, in the meantime, had enough to suffer when placed under the authority of such a wicked woman. She was removed from the rooms which she and her father had occupied, when the old couple took possession of them.

There was plenty of room in the farm house, but she was lodged in the most uncomfortable garret. Her new employer seemed to take a pleasure in tormenting her; she gave her the meanest work to do, and delighted in venting her own evil temper in scolding her. Nothing Mary could do would please. The poor old couple pitied her, but they were unable to help her, except by their sympathy. In her distress she consulted the good minister of Erlenbrünnen. He said to her, "It is evident, my poor girl, that the Pine Farm is no longer a proper home for you. You have received an excellent education, and this is wasted where you are now. You are losing your time in doing the ordinary coarse work of a farm, and such work is beyond your strength, and will hurt your health. I will do all in my power to find a more suitable home for you, and I hope to be able to do so before long, but in the meantime, my poor Mary, pray to God to give you strength to bear your hard lot patiently, and do not hastily try to escape from it, till his providence opens a way for you. He who has fitted you for a better place, will remove you to it in his own good time. Trust in him. Commit thy way unto the Lord, trust also in him, and he shall bring it to pass.' (Psalms 37:5.) Be assured that I will do all in my power for you."

Mary thanked the good minister, and promised to follow his advice.

The only place the poor girl had now any peace, was at her father's grave. She planted a rose-bush by it. It was leafless when she planted it; it had nothing on it but thorns; but it soon began to bud and blossom, and in a little time it was in full blow. Mary remembered one of her father's lessons. I will wait patiently said she, this is my time of thorns, but perhaps I shall yet see the fulfillment of the proverb: "Time brings roses."

Chapter Fourteen

WANDERING AGAIN

TIME wore on, for even the saddest days have an end, and the 25th of July came round, the anniversary of James's birthday. In all former years, this day had been a kind of celebration to Mary, a day when she was accustomed to bring a gift to her dear father of the finest flowers in her garden, and sometimes she added to this some little piece of work which she prepared for him as a pleasant surprise. Oh, how she wished that he were still beside her to smile on her offerings! Poor Mary! this anniversary was now a day of peculiar suffering. She could do nothing for her dear father now—he was gone forever from her cares on earth. But the peasants at Erlenbrünnen had a custom of ornamenting the tombs of those they loved with garlands, and Mary on that melancholy day took a fancy to carry her former offering of flowers to her father's grave. She took the basket, the cause and the memorial of all her suffering, and having filled it with the finest flowers she could procure, she carried it to the churchyard, and laid it on her father's grave. "I cannot raise a tombstone to my beloved father," said she, "I have nothing to put over his grave but this basket, the only beautiful thing I possess." She left it on the grave, and no one ventured to remove it. The simple villagers who saw it sympathized with the poor orphan, and considered her gift as sacred.

The day after this melancholy anniversary, as the workers of the farm were returning, as usual, from their work in the fields, where they had been busy making hay, they found their mistress in one of her most fearful fits of passion. A piece of linen that had been laid out in the sun to bleach had disappeared and she was furious. She had heard the story of the ring, for honest James, truthful in all things, had told the whole history to the old farmer and his wife. They had told their son, and he had imprudently confided it to his wife. In consequence of this, her suspicions instantly fell upon Mary. When the poor weary girl appeared in the evening with her rake on her shoulder, worn out by her day's labor, she was met by the furious woman, who demanded, with a torrent of abuse, where she had put the linen which she had undoubtedly stolen. Mary meekly answered that it was impossible that she could have taken the linen, since she had been the whole day in the hayfield with the other workers, and had not been a moment alone. But she reminded her mistress that as all the people on the farm were busy with the hay, any stranger or wandering beggar might have easily stolen the linen unobserved. This had really been the case, but the angry woman refused to listen to reason. She exclaimed in a fury, "Thief that you are! you have escaped from justice before: if you had had your due, you would have been hanged long ago. Get out of my sight, you wretch! you shall not spend another night under my roof."

At this point her husband tried to interpose; "There is no proof that the girl is guilty—we cannot not send her away so late; it is already dark. Let her have a supper, since she worked so hard all day, and she will stay for this night at least."

"Not for an hour!" replied the miserable woman, "and hold you your tongue— or I will stop your mouth for you in a way you will not like."

The poor weak man was silent. Having once been foolish enough to yield to his wife, he could not regain his authority. The man who is weak enough to let his wife rule at first, becomes in time her slave, and is degraded in the eyes of others and in his own. If a man is foolish enough to marry an unprincipled woman who does not know her duty, he at least ought to do his,—to take the authority which God has given him, to be master from the first, and to restrain the wife who is committed to his care and guidance. The farmer's son had not spirit enough to do this. He had never restrained his wife. He had allowed her to ill-treat his own parents, and it was not likely that she would yield to him now. Poor Mary knew her master's weakness: she felt that his intercession would be of no avail, so she at once prepared to depart. She tied up her few possessions in a small bundle, which was not a heavy one, and she then asked her mistress to allow her to delay a few minutes, that she might bid farewell to the kind old couple.

"Oh, go and see them if you like," said she scornfully, "you seem to suit each other mighty well. I only wish you would take them with you, for Death seems to have forgotten them, or to think them not worth coming for."

The good old people had heard all that had passed, and were waiting to receive Mary. They expected that she would come to bid them good-bye, and they consoled her as well as they could. They had little to give, but they gave her all they had, a few florins for her expenses till she could find work.

"Dear child," said they, "we would keep you with us if we dared: you know we cannot; but God will be with you and bless you. He was with your father, and he will not forsake you. Happiness is in store for you yet."

Mary, with her little bundle in her hand, left the farm and took the road that led to the churchyard. She wished to visit her father's grave once more. It was getting dark as she reached the church, but she did not feel the slightest fear at going thus among the tombs. She fell prostrate on the grave, and wept bitterly. All was silent, except the gentle rustling of the evening breeze among the leaves.

"Oh my father! my father!" said poor Mary, "how I miss you now! The last time we were cast out homeless, I felt cheerful because you were with me. What shall I do? Where shall I go now? I have never been so wretched. Even in prison, though you were not with me, I hoped to see you again. I knew you were thinking of me, suffering with me, praying for me, watching the moment to come to me. Oh that I had you again! But no, it is wrong to wish this. I ought rather to be thankful that you have not been spared to see this miserable day. Where shall I go? I do not know even where to seek shelter for the night. If I go to any house in the village, they will ask why I have left the farm, and when they hear the reason, they will not take me in. Oh God, have mercy on me! Take me out of this world, or give me strength to bear and to suffer with patience." She looked sadly round her, and she saw near her an old tombstone covered with moss, a little raised above the damp earth. "I will sit down on this stone," said she, "and wait for the daylight. God will protect me. I will then go to another village where my story is not known, and ask for work. Perhaps this may be the last time that I shall be able to sit by my father's grave."

"Mourner, who sittest in the churchyard lone,
Scanning the lines on that marble stone,
Plucking the weeds from thy loved one's bed,
Planting the myrtle and rose instead,
Look up from the tomb with thy tearful eye,
'Jesus of Nazareth' passeth by.

"Stranger, afar from thy native land,
Whom no man takes with a brother's hand,
Table and hearthstone are glowing free,
Casements are sparkling, but not for thee
There is One can tell of a home on high,
'Jesus of Nazareth' passeth by."

Chapter Fifteen

HELP APPEARS OUT OF NOWHERE

MARY sat down on the moss-covered stone near the wall, under the dark shade of the fir trees, and hid her face in her hands. She prayed earnestly to God for strength and help. At length she thought she heard a gentle voice calling, "Mary! Mary!" She started up, and saw in the twilight a beautiful figure standing near her, dressed in white. Mary, surprised at the sudden apparition, exclaimed, "Has God indeed sent one of his angels to help me?"

"I am no angel, dear Mary," said the gentle voice; "I am a human being like yourself, but I am come to help you. God has heard your prayers, and sent me to you. you not know me, dear Mary? Do you not remember Amelia?"

"Yes," said Mary, "it is indeed you, my dear lady; but how did you come here? How is it possible that you are alone, at this hour, in this lonely churchyard, so far from your home?"

Amelia embraced her tenderly, and sitting down on the tombstone, drew Mary gently to her side. "It is a long story, dear Mary, but you shall hear it all in time. I must first tell you, however, how glad I am that I have found you—how sorry we all are that you were unjustly blamed. We discovered your innocence too late. Oh, how ill we all behaved to you! What a poor return I made you for your kindness in bringing me the pretty basket! Can you forgive us, dear Mary? We are most anxious to do all we can to atone for our injustice. Will you forgive us?"

"Oh, do not speak of pardon or of injustice, dear lady," said Mary, "you were justified in suspecting me, the evidence against me seemed so strong, and you behaved kindly and gently, believing as you did that I was guilty. I have never felt any resentment to you or to your noble parents. I have only remembered your kindness. But one thing continued to pain me, and that was, that you should still believe me guilty and ungrateful. I often prayed earnestly that God would be pleased to make manifest my innocence, and now he has heard my prayer. You believe me innocent, and I am happy."

Amelia kissed Mary again, and praised her for her gentle and forgiving spirit; then, casting her eyes on the grave, she said bitterly, "Oh, there is an injustice for which we cannot atone. Worthy, excellent old man! how could we suspect you? Your long and faithful service should have placed you above suspicion. You made the cradle in which I first slept, and your last work at Eichbourg was this basket for my birthday present. Your whole life was spent in our service, and how did we repay it?—by suspicion, and distrust, and ingratitude! Oh, if we had not been so rash in judging,—if we had but been charitable, if we had thought the best,—if we had refused to believe that such an old faithful servant as you could shield dishonesty even in your own child, perhaps you might still have been with us, respected and happy, and your poor daughter would have been spared all this agony. Oh, Mary, when I think how we have injured you, I scarcely know what to say; but if kindness can atone for it, you shall never know want or suffering more. Did your father forgive us, dear Mary? Did he ever speak of us?"

"My dear lady," said Mary, "believe me, my father never felt the least resentment towards you. He always said you had acted gently, believing us guilty, and that you had reason to think so from the evidence. I assure you that he never forgot to pray for you, as he always had done at Eichbourg. He often spoke of you. He said that he was sure that sooner or later you would find out that we were innocent, and that you would recall us from banishment. "If I do not live to see that day," said he to me, "you will tell the young Countess Amelia how much I always loved her. I carried her in my arms when she was a little child: I know her amiable disposition: I am sure she will grieve deeply when she discovers that we have been falsely accused."

Amelia wept bitterly on hearing these words. At last she said, "Generous old man, how I honor him! Here, by his grave, dear Mary, I must tell you how God sent me to help you."

Chapter Sixteen

AMELIA EXPLAINS HER SUDDEN APPEARANCE

"GOD is with you of a truth, dear Mary," said Amelia," for his providence is clearly to be seen in all the circumstances which have brought me here exactly at the right moment to help you. Ever since I discovered that you were innocent, I have tried anxiously to find you, but in vain. You were ever present to my thoughts, and I could not rest without finding you, to tell you that you are quite cleared from suspicion, without doing all I could to atone to you for all you had so undeservedly suffered. My father tried every means to discover where you had gone, but all our inquiries were fruitless. A few days ago we came to this neighborhood, because my father, who is keeper of the king's forests, had some business to settle about the woods in this part of the country. He has been busy all day about this matter, along with two other noblemen, who are also concerned in it. Since we came here, we have been living in a hunting-lodge belonging to the king, and these two other noblemen, with their wives, are also there. This evening my mother was obliged to remain in the drawing-room to entertain these ladies; but the evening was so beautiful, so cool, and so inviting, that I begged her permission to take a ramble to see the neighborhood. My mother allowed me to go a little way, and sent the forester's daughter with me to show me anything worth seeing. She took me through the village, and as we passed the church, the gate of the churchyard was standing open. I have always had a fancy for reading the inscriptions on tombstones. I went into the churchyard, followed by the forester's daughter, who, willing apparently to humor my fancies, said,

'The only grave worth seeing in this churchyard is that of a poor man who died lately. It has neither tombstone nor inscription, but his daughter has adorned it with a beautiful basket of flowers. Would you like to see it?' I followed where she guided me, and judge of my surprise when I saw the basket—the very basket that had been the cause of so much suffering! I was sure it was the same, for I saw my own name and crest upon it. I eagerly asked the girl to tell me all she knew about you and your father. She told me of your being at the Pine Farm, of your father's illness and death, and of your grief. I immediately went to the minister's house, which I thought the most likely place to hear more of you. I found the minister a worthy old man, who gave you a very high character. I wished to go at once to the Pine Farm, but the minister advised me not to attempt it, saying that it was too far off, and as I had delayed some time conversing with him, it was now so late that it would be dark before I could get there. What shall I do, then,' said I, 'for we leave this place tomorrow as early as possible?'

The good minister sent for the sexton, and desired him to go as quickly as he could to the farm, and to bring you with him to the parsonage. 'I need not go so far to find the poor girl,' said the sexton, 'for a few minutes ago, as I went to wind up the church clock, I saw her go into the churchyard. I have no doubt she is there now, weeping as usual at her father's grave.' On hearing this, I resolved to return immediately here. The good minister offered to come with me, but I wished our first meeting to be alone. I begged him rather to be so good as to go to the hunting lodge, where my father and my mother would be very glad to see him, to relieve my mother's anxiety about my long absence, and to tell her of my having found you. He agreed to do so, and I came here. You see now, dear Mary, how I appeared so suddenly at your side, and thus the basket has been the cause of our meeting again."

"Yes," said Mary, clasping her hands, and raising her eyes in thankfulness to heaven, "God has graciously done this. He has heard my prayers, he has seen my tears. Oh, how merciful he is! The Bible says that he sends his angels to help his people, and I think he also sends angels in human form to bring consolation to the afflicted."

Amelia interrupted her, saying, "Do not speak in this way of me, dear Mary; I am no angel, but God can use any instrument he pleases. I must tell you one thing more of his providence in this matter. Do you remember Margaret? You know she was jealous of you, and did not hesitate to invent the most odious falsehoods to deprive you of our favor, and to separate you from me. For a short time she appeared to triumph, and, glorying in her wickedness, she took the basket, and without any orders from us to do so, she threw it at your feet as you passed the castle. She then thought she had got rid of you forever, but this very piece of malignity has been the means, in the providence of God, of reuniting us, for the basket has been the cause of my finding you here. If it had not been for this basket on the grave, I might have gone away without ever hearing of you, though we were so near each other.

Is it not true that God brings good out of evil? Margaret has been found out and punished, and I have another maid now who is very different, for she is a pious woman—a true Christian. Through her means, dear Mary, I have learned to know the truth, and to love the Bible. I think even your good father would not be so much afraid to trust you with me now. But after I have said so much about ourselves, tell me, my poor Mary, how you came to be sitting so late by the grave alone."

Mary then related all that had passed at the farm that evening, and her distress.

"Oh!" exclaimed the young Countess, "here is another wonder of God's providence. He sent me just at your utmost need, and this wicked woman's cruelty in sending you away was the cause of our meeting sooner than we otherwise might have done. But we must not sit here much longer: it is getting very late, and my father and mother are expecting me. Come, then, Mary, you shall go with me: we are not to be parted again."

Mary cast one last look at the grave, which she thought she might never see again. Amelia observed it, and said kindly, "Come, Mary, bring the basket: we will keep it as a remembrance of your good old father, and instead of it I will order a tombstone to be erected, which will be a more lasting monument. Come, then; you shall return here some time soon, and in the meantime I must tell you the story of the finding of the ring, while we are walking home."

The moon had now risen, and by its pleasant light the two girls saw their way out of the churchyard. At the gate they found the forester's daughter waiting, with a servant whom the Countess had sent to accompany them to the hunting-lodge.

Chapter Seventeen

THE RING REAPPEARS

A LONG avenue of lime trees led to the hunting-lodge, and as Amelia and Mary walked along this, Amelia told the story of the finding of the ring— "Last year," said she, "we left the court sooner than usual, on account of business which required my father's presence at Eichbourg, and we arrived there about the beginning of March. The weather was cold and stormy, and one night in particular, it blew a perfect hurricane. Do you remember the large old pear tree that was in our garden? It was very old indeed, and scarcely bore any fruit. The wind shook it that night to such a degree, that it seemed ready to fall every moment. My father ordered it to be cut down, lest it should fall and do harm. All the servants of the castle were called to assist at the time, that its fall might be managed so as not to hurt the trees that were near it. My father and mother, and all of us, went to the garden to see it cut down, for we were all much interested in the fall of such an old friend. Scarcely was it down, when my two little brothers rushed eagerly to seize a magpie's nest that was in one of the branches near the top, which they had often coveted while it was beyond their reach. 'What is this?' exclaimed Augustus. 'What can this be, shining so bright among the little sticks of which the nest is made?'

'It is sparkling like gold and diamonds,' said Alfred. Margaret, who was present, went forward as soon as she heard this, and no sooner had she seen it, than she uttered an involuntary cry, 'It is the ring! it is the ring!' She then suddenly became deadly pale, and trembled all over. In the meantime, the boys pulled out the ring from the nest, and carried it to my mother with shouts of triumph. 'It is indeed the ring which I lost,' said my mother. 'Oh, good honest James! Oh, poor Mary! what grievous wrong we have done her!—how we have misjudged the poor innocent! I am certainly very glad to find my ring, but I am now much more anxious to find the good gardener and his daughter. I would give ten times the value of the ring, to have it in my power to atone in any measure for the wrong we have done them. But how could this ring have got to the very top of this old tree?'

'That is easily understood,' said old Anthony the forester, whose face was perfectly beaming with delight at hearing your innocence acknowledged. You know, Mary, he never would believe anything against you. 'It is easy to see,' continued he, that neither James nor Mary could have hid it up there, the tree was too high, and the branches too weak for anyone to get at that nest till the tree was down. The young gentlemen have tried it often enough to be quite sure of that. It is one of these thievish birds, the magpies, who has stolen the ring. They have an odd fancy for everything shining, and they have been known to carry money to their nests, or anything bright or sparkling that came in their way. There is nothing at all wonderful in their having stolen the ring, the only wonder is, that an old woodman like me should not have thought of this before. Surely it was an extraordinary piece of blindness never once to have thought of it, when this tree was so near the window too. It shows that it has been the will of God to send this trial to my good old friend James, and his innocent daughter, or we could never all have been so stupid.' 'You are right, Anthony,' said my mother, 'it seems all clear enough now. I remember perfectly that these magpies had a custom of visiting my window, and even of coming into the room. It was a very warm day when I lost the ring. The window was open, and the ring was on the table, near the open window where I had been sitting. There is no doubt now of the truth, that one of these birds, attracted by the sparkling of the diamonds, had carried off the ring while I was in the next room.' My father listened in surprise. How is it,' said he, that we did not think of this sooner? I am grieved to the very heart for all that we have made these good innocent people suffer. My only consolation in the matter is, that, at least, I intended to act justly and uprightly: my conscience is clear from any evil intention towards them. But that will not justify our too hasty judgment. I shall have no peace till we find them again, and restore them to their country, and their home, and do all in our power to atone, in every way, for their unmerited sufferings.' Turning round at this moment, my father perceived Margaret, who stood listening to this conversation, almost stupified with terror.

She looked as if she were frozen to the spot. Her guilt was written on her face. 'Wicked and deceitful woman,' said my father to her, how could you perjure yourself as you must have done at the trial, and so not only sin most grievously yourself, but become the means of leading us all into sin likewise, for but for your false evidence Mary would never have been condemned. You shall not escape unpunished; seize her,' said he to some of the servants, and take her at once to the police officer, she must be given into custody for perjury.' Margaret was no favorite in the household, and there were none to pity her. 'It is quite right,' said one of the servants, 'that the person who lays snares for others, should be taken in their own net.' "This is the end of her cheating and lying,' said another, 'she has deceived my lady long enough, it is a good thing she is found out at last. It is a true saying, there is no thread so fine that it cannot be seen in the sunshine.' The cook said, 'This has all come of her jealousy about Mary's pretty dress. It just shows how far one bad feeling, indulged, may lead a person. Her jealousy led her to lying, and fear for her lies being found out, led her to perjure herself. It is a true word, that if we give the devil but a single hair to hold by, he will drag us down by it to destruction.' 'Well,' said the coachmen, still holding the axe with which he had been helping to cut the pear tree, we must hope that she will repent, or it will be the worse for her in the next world, for,' continued he, shaking the axe, 'it is written, that "every tree that brings not forth good fruit, shall be hewn down and cast into the fire." I may as well tell you at once," continued Amelia, what became of Margaret. "She was condemned to lose all the money she had amassed in our service, most of which had been got dishonestly. All she had was taken from her; she was banished, and actually escorted across the frontier by the very police officer who formerly accompanied you.

"The news of the discovery of the ring spread rapidly in the village, and many came to inquire into the particulars of it, and to see the tree. The judge who condemned you, dear Mary, heard of it from the officer who took Margaret to prison, and he hastened immediately to the castle. You could scarcely believe how deeply he felt it. He was in very great distress about you, for though a stern and rigid man, he is strictly just. 'I would give the half of my fortune,' said he, nay! I would give all that I possess that these innocent people had not been condemned. It is very dreadful to have been the instrument of condemning the innocent unjustly.' Then turning to the crowd who had collected near the fallen tree, he said solemnly; 'God is the only judge who can never be deceived, because he alone sees the heart. All human judges are fallible, and may err, and therefore it is not uncommon for innocent people to suffer unjustly in this world.

In some cases, this may never be discovered till the great day, when the secrets of all hearts shall be revealed. But in this instance, God has been graciously pleased to clear the innocent, and punish the guilty, even in this world. Remark and admire, my friends, by what a singular train of little unforeseen circumstances it has pleased God to bring about this discovery, and if one of these little events in the chain had been wanting, the discovery might not have been made. First, the Count was brought here by business during the stormy season, contrary to his usual custom, or he might not have been here at the fall of the tree, then the storm was sent to shake the old tree to its roots—the torrents of rain were necessary, too, to clean the nest, and make the ring visible—the presence of the children was necessary to seize the nest directly, and prevent anyone else from finding the ring, who might have hid it—then Margaret, the false accuser, was brought to the spot at the moment, and by her own involuntary cry, was made the first to acknowledge the identity of the ring, and consequently, the innocence of her victims. Much of the wrong and injustice that fill the earth will never be known, or punished, till the great day of judgment; but from time to time, God permits such instances, as we have seen today, for a warning to the wicked, that they cannot deceive their all-seeing Judge; and for an encouragement to his people, who, amid the multiplied injustice that prevails all around them, might become faint-hearted, and be tempted to lose their trust in his eternal truth and justice.'" Thus spoke the judge in an authoritative tone, and the crowd listened with approval to his words, and then quietly dispersed.

"And this is all the story, dear Mary, about the finding of the ring." Just as Amelia had finished her story, they reached the door of the hunting-lodge.

Chapter Eighteen

ATONEMENT FOR INJUSTICE

In the meantime, the Count and Countess and the other ladies and gentlemen of their party, were assembled in the great drawing-room. According to the old German fashion, this room was hung with very fine tapestry, on which was depicted, with great art and skill, a succession of hunting scenes, with huntsmen, dogs, horses, stags, and wild boars. Notwithstanding the great antiquity of this tapestry, the colors were still bright and fresh, and when the room was lighted up in the evening, it had a very fine effect. The good minister of Erlenbrünnen was among the party assembled there that evening. According to the Countess Amelia's request, he had gone to the hunting-lodge to relieve her mother's mind about her long absence, when she went to find Mary, and he had been invited to remain to supper. He had been hearing from the Countess, with much interest, a similar account to that which Amelia had been giving to Mary, and he had related to her in return many little circumstances which interested her most deeply about good old James, his blameless and useful life, and his happy death. When he told of Mary's patience in affliction, her unwearied care of her father, her industry, her activity, her gentleness, and her most unmerited sufferings since her father's death, he brought tears to the eyes of all who heard him, and prepared them all to receive Mary with the utmost kindness.

When the Countess Amelia entered the drawing-room, leading in Mary with one hand, and carrying in the other the basket of flowers; all the company gathered round them, and Mary was welcomed by all present. The Count took her kindly by the hand and said, "Poor girl, how pale and thin you look. It grieves me to see you look so ill, especially when I remember that it was our rash judging, and too hasty decision which has made you suffer, and changed you so fearfully. Please forgive us, and we will do all we can to bring the roses back to your cheeks, and to make you like yourself again. We drove you unjustly from your old home, but now it shall be your own property. I give you the house where you formerly lived, and the garden and orchard you were so fond of; my secretary shall draw out a deed of gift; I will sign it this very evening, and Amelia shall have the pleasure of presenting it to you."

The Countess kissed Mary, and taking from her finger the ring which had caused so much sorrow, she slipped it on Mary's finger, saying kindly, "My dear Mary, you do not need gold and jewels, for your ornaments are of a much more valuable kind, but notwithstanding, it will give me pleasure if you will accept this ring and keep it as a mark of my affection for you, and of my earnest wish to make any compensation in my power for the injustice we have done you. If it is not of much use to you as an ornament, it may serve at least for your marriage portion, when you need one. Wear it till then, dear Mary, and if a time comes when you require a dowry, and when money would be more valuable to you, I promise to redeem it then for more than its value."

Mary was so overcome by all she had gone through that day, her fatigue and misery at the farm, her anguish in the churchyard, and the sudden and overwhelming change to hope, and joy, and happiness, that she could not utter one word. It seemed as if she were hesitating to accept the Countess's gift.

"Take the ring, my good girl," said one of the gentlemen guests, never refuse a generous gift. The noble Countess has a benevolent heart, and she is rich enough to indulge her kindly feelings."

"Do not flatter me, Baron," said the Countess; "it is not generous in you to do so. We do not desire to be called benevolent for what we are now doing. What we do for Mary is simply justice, and it is owed her, not a matter of our generosity. We have done a public act of injustice, of which I cannot think without shame, and our honor and our peace of mind require that it should be publicly acknowledged and recompense be made for the harm we caused."

Poor Mary, uncertain what to do, confused and bewildered, held in her hand the beautiful ring which she had taken off her finger, and looking round the party for her kind friend and adviser, the good old minister, she seemed to ask him, with her expressive eyes, whether she should take it or not.

"Yes, Mary," said the worthy man, kindly replying to her mute question, "it is right for you to accept this jewel. It was the cause of your sorrow, it will be the public symbol now of your entire vindication. It would hurt the Countess if you were to refuse what she has proffered to make amends. Take it, then, my child, and may God grant that you may be as gentle, humble, and pious in prosperity as you have been patient, meek, and resigned in adversity."

Mary hesitated no longer; she put the ring on her finger, and gently kissed the Countess's hand, but she could not speak for tears.

The Countess Amelia had been a delighted spectator of the whole scene. Her eyes sparkled with joy at seeing her parents so kind to Mary.

The minister noticed this with approbation. He had too often seen the envious spirit with which young people sometimes react at the praises of others, especially from their own parents. But not one spark of envy or jealousy was entertained by the good-hearted Amelia. She was quite willing to take second place while Mary was being honored, and allow Mary to be engrossed in the attention of all the company,—forgetting herself entirely, and considering only Mary.

[Young readers, consider your reactions to other peoples' successes, blessings and joys. Do you feel genuine happiness when a friend receives praise or attention, even if you're not the focus? Can you sincerely celebrate when someone else wins an award or achieves more than you?

Reflect on how you handle situations where others outshine you in popularity, accomplishments, or esteem. It's natural to feel competitive, but true maturity involves finding joy in others' successes.

Consider the wisdom in this biblical guidance: "Look not every man on his own things, but every man also on the things of others" (Phil. 2:4). This teaches us to care about others' well-being as much as our own.

Have you embraced the empathy the Bible encourages? Do you practice the principle to "rejoice with them that do rejoice, and weep with them that weep" (Rom. 12:15)?

These questions can help you develop a more compassionate and selfless outlook, fostering stronger relationships and personal growth.]

Chapter Nineteen

AN EVENING AT THE HUNTING LODGE

WHEN supper was announced, the Countess invited Mary to accompany them to the dining room. Mary would have modestly declined, but the Countess would take no refusal, and she insisted on placing Mary at table between herself and her daughter. When Mary was crossing the hall with the rest of the company to go to the dining room, she could not help thinking on the strange change that had taken place in her circumstances in so short a time. She had been dismissed in disgrace from the Pine Farm, and thought unworthy to share in the laborers' supper, and she now found herself an honored guest at a nobleman's table. God can in a moment work these changes in the position of anyone; He casteth down, and he raiseth up, "He raiseth up the poor out of the dust, and lifteth the needy out of the dunghill, that he may set him with princes, even with the princes of the people." (Psalm 113:7, 8,) Therefore, let none despair, for God can raise them as suddenly as he cast them down; and let none murmur, because he has chosen their position for them, whatever it may be.

When the party were all arranged at table, the good minister asked a blessing. While Mary sat bewildered, wondering if it were not all a dream, her story was much talked of by the company.

Old Anthony was present among the servants in waiting. He had been brought by the Count on this occasion, because of his knowledge of the woods in the neighborhood, and his experience was required in settling the point in dispute. He was a privileged person, on account of his age and his long services, and he took more liberty than would have been permitted to anyone else. Even while waiting at table, he could not refrain from congratulating his old favorite Mary, in a low voice, on the happy change in her fortunes, and he showed his special interest in her by keeping much behind her chair. He even ventured to whisper to her, "Oh that your worthy father had lived to see this day!"

The good minister overheard the remark, and feeling interested in the beaming, joyous face of the kindly old man, he indirectly replied to it.

"Mary's good father," said he, "would have rejoiced to hear her innocence publicly acknowledged; but we cannot, even for a moment, wish him back again among us. He is gone to be with Christ, which is far better. It has been God's will to take James away before any public atonement could be made to him for his sufferings; but God knows best, and chooses the best for each of his people. What is any atonement that could have been made to him here, compared to the unfading glories, the unmixed joys of the paradise above? It pleases God, in some instances, to raise the afflicted even in this world from the dust, and to restore to them the cup of earthly happiness which has been dashed from their lips, as he did in the case of Job; but in other instances, it pleases him that the mourner should suffer during the whole of his pilgrimage below, as in the case of Lazarus. We know not why he so orders events: we only know that whatever he orders is wisest and best. We cannot understand this now. He himself has said, "What I do thou knowest not now, but thou shalt know hereafter;" and this ought to answer every question on the subject that may arise in our minds."

"Perhaps," continued the minister, "I may be permitted to mention a curious coincidence which took place during James's last illness, which may show that though he was not permitted to live to see this happy day, he nevertheless died with the assured hope that it would come, and enjoyed it, if I may so speak, by anticipation. One day, when I went to see him, he appeared even more than usually cheerful. His countenance was actually beaming with joy. I have slept little last night, sir,' he said, and I spent the sleepless hours in earnest prayer. I have been strengthened to pray as I never prayed before; and such peace has been shed abroad in my soul that every doubt and fear have vanished. Before this, I have sometimes had uneasy thoughts about my darling child, but now my mind is at ease. I have trusted her to God. I feel sure, quite sure, that her innocence will be publicly acknowledged, and that God will raise up friends to her when I am gone; perhaps even the very friends we have lost, who will care for her and provide for her better than I could have done had I been spared to her.' It is a strange coincidence which I have traced since I came here tonight, that the storm which shook the pear tree and caused the finding of the ring, took place on the very night which my old friend spent in prayer. The Countess told me tonight the exact date; and from some circumstances which kept it in my mind, I remembered that this date was the same as that of James's prayer. It is a remarkable instance of the power of prayer. God hears the prayers of his people, and sometimes answers them, even while the suppliant is unconscious, except by faith in His promise, that the answer has been actually vouchsafed."

The Countess now gave the signal for rising from table, and as she rose she said to the old minister, "After all that you have said of the efficacy of prayer, we must not separate without asking God's blessing, and thanking him for his goodness to us this day. If you will be so good as to accompany me, I shall order the household to be assembled in the library; our guests, I am sure will join us, and I hope you will pray with us before you go home."

The good minister gladly consented, and thus the day was closed. He offered up an impressive prayer, and the party separated for the night.

Chapter Twenty

A VISIT TO THE PINE FARM

EARLY next morning all was bustle in the hunting-lodge, for the whole party were preparing to depart. The Countess Amelia, as considerate as kind, knocked at the door of Mary's room before she was dressed. "I come to tell you, dear Mary," said she, "not to dress till my maid brings you a complete set of my things. She has not brought many of my dresses, as we did not intend to stay long here, but she will find something or other fit for you to wear in the meantime. You may trust yourself safely in her hands; she is a good creature, not at all like Margaret, and she will see that you are properly fitted, at least as well as time will permit. You must not wear this peasant's dress any longer, dear Mary, for, now you are to remain always with me, your dress must be suitable to your new situation, and it is better the change should be made at once, before we go to Eichbourg. It will excite less remark."

Mary came down to breakfast, dressed in her new attire, and looked so remarkably well in it, that the visitors barely recognized her. After breakfast they set off, and the Count ordered the coachman to stop at the Pine Farm, which was but a little way off the road. On the way the Count questioned Mary about the people at the farm; he was anxious to recompense them in some way for their kindness to old James; and Mary told him how unhappy the poor old couple were.

The arrival of the Count's carriage at the farm produced a great sensation, for never had such an equipage been seen at the door before. The young farmer's wife came out in great haste, anxious to do all honor to such noble visitors. She was as servile to those above her, as tyrannical to those under her authority, for these two things are always united. She officiously offered her services to help the ladies to alight; but what was her surprise when, as she was carefully protecting the dress of one of the ladies from the mud on the wheel, she perceived that she was giving herself all this trouble for Mary. Surprised out of her assumed good manners, she started back, and forgetting her noble guests, she exclaimed, "What can this mean?" and rushed off to find her husband, without waiting to be spoken to. Conscience stricken, she feared they had come to punish her for her cruelty.

As she disappeared, the Count saw the old farmer working in the garden, and, accompanied by the ladies, he went to speak to him. He thanked him for his kindness to James and Mary.

Indeed, my lord," said the honest farmer, "the obligation was all the other way. I owe more to good old James than I ever had it in my power to do for him. This garden was an uncultivated wilderness when he came, and your Excellency sees what a pretty place he has made of it. It is a pleasure to me to keep it now, and I make a good penny too by the fruit since he pruned the trees and put them all in order. I am never so happy as when I am working here, trying to keep it as he left it, and thinking of the good advice he often gave me in this very place."

While the farmer was speaking to the Count, Mary had gone to find his wife. She insisted on bringing her to see her new friends, assuring her that she need not feel afraid of them, they were so kind and good.

The good old woman was kindly received, and thanked also for her affectionate care of Mary. The worthy farmer and his wife rejoiced truly in Mary's good fortune.

"Your father's words have come true," said they; "he always said that God would provide friends for you. His favorite saying, 'He who clothes the lilies will also clothe us,' has been fulfilled."

In the meantime, the young farmer's wife had overcome her first panic, but still kept at a little distance, overwhelmed with envy and rage. "Well, well," muttered she, some people have good luck who don't deserve it. Here is a miserable beggar changed all at once into a lady. These great lords and ladies do take strange whims! What could have made them take a fancy to such a creature, and dress her up as they have done? For my part, I never could bear the sight of her. They will soon tire of her, I dare say, and turn her out again. At any rate, dress her as they may, she will always be known for what she is, a poor creature taken in out of charity."

The Count did not hear these words, but he observed the woman's manner, and read in her face her malignant temper. He thought for a moment; then he said to the old farmer, "I have an offer to make you, my good friend, which I hope you will accept. I have just given to Mary the house and garden which her father rented at Eichbourg, but as my daughter wishes to keep her with herself, and as, besides, she is too young yet to live there alone, what do you say to taking possession of it? I am sure you will like it, and I think I can promise, in Mary's name, that she will not ask any rent from you. You can indulge your taste for flowers there as much as you like, and think of your old friend too, for you will find many at Eichbourg who remember his counsels, and will be glad to talk of him."

The Count's wife, Amelia and Mary joined in urging the old man to accept this generous offer. But there was no need for persuasion. The old people were happy to be taken from their uncomfortable surroundings, and gladly agreed to the proposal.

At this moment the young farmer came home from the fields. His surprise was as great as his wife's when he saw the carriage at his door drawn by four white horses; for never in the history of the farm had a carriage stopped there before. When he heard of the proposal which the Count had made to his father and mother, he gladly consented to it, although he was deeply grieved to part from his old parents. His consolation was found, however, in thinking that they were going to be happier than they could possibly be with his wretched wife.

As for his wife herself, the only remark she made was to say in a spiteful way to the Count—

"It is a great favor you are doing us in ridding us of two old people who are nothing but a burden!"

Promising to send for the old farmer and his wife as soon as everything was ready, the Count and his family, accompanied by Mary, now entered the carriage and drove off.

Chapter Twenty One

RETRIBUTION

In course of time, when arrangements had been made for their reception, a carriage was sent from Eichbourg to bring away the old farmer and his wife. Their son was grieved to the heart when the time came for them to go, but their daughter-in-law had counted the days and hours until the time of their departure, and felt nothing but vindictive pleasure at being rid of them. Her joy, however, received a severe check from a note which the coachman presented to her, in which the Count informed her that she and her husband should pay all that had been stipulated for the support of her father and mother-in-law; and that the price of their living valued in money, according to the current market price, should be paid to them every quarter. Realizing her helplessness, she became violently angry and turned round to her husband, saying, "We have been outdone! If they had stayed here, it would not have cost us half as much." Her husband was secretly pleased to think that he was still permitted to help his parents in their old age, but he took good care not to show his joy before his wife.

The old people set off in the carriage the next morning, followed by the blessings of their son and the secret ill-wishes of their daughter-in-law.

But the unnatural conduct of this wicked woman was visited with the trouble which is always the lot of avarice and inhumanity. Her secretly-cherished god was gold, and she had lent the bulk of her money to a merchant to use in his business, on his promise to pay her a large interest for the loan. Her greatest pleasure was in making calculations, as to how much her money would amount to after a certain number of years, with all the interest and compound interest added. Suddenly, however, these golden dreams received a rude awakening. The manufacturer's speculations proved unfortunate, and he shortly afterwards failed in business, and his goods were sold by order of the sheriff.

The news came as a thunder clap for the farmer's wife, and from the moment that she heard of the catastrophe she had no repose. Every day she kept running to the lawyers, or to her neighbors to complain of her hard lot, and the nights she spent in weeping and scolding her husband. From the wreck of her fortune of ten thousand florins she received only a paltry hundred or two, and so deeply did she feel the loss of her money that she openly declared her wish to die. The result of the continual worrying induced a fever which never left her. When her husband wished to send for a physician she would not consent to it, and when, in spite of her objections, he at last sent for one, his wife in a passion threw the medicine he prescribed out of the window.

At last her husband saw that she was seriously ill, and he requested the minister of Erlenbrunn to come and see her. The good old man visited her frequently and talked to her affectionately, in order to induce her to repent of her sins, and to detach her heart from the things of this earth, that she might turn to God.

But this advice made her very angry. She looked at the good man with utter astonishment. "I do not know," she said, "for what purpose the minister comes to preach repentance to me. He should have delivered such a sermon to the merchant who stole our money. Yes, there would have been some sense in that. As for me, I do not see that I have any reason for repentance. As long as I was able to go out I always went to church, and I have never failed to say my prayers. I have not ceased all my life to do my duty and to behave myself like a virtuous housewife. I defy any living soul to slander me. And of all the poor people who have come to my door, not one can complain that I sent them away without giving them something. Now, I should like to know how any one can behave better!"

The venerable pastor saw that she was justifying herself before God, and he tried by adopting a more direct tone to lead her to contrition. He showed to her that she loved money more than anything else in the world, and that the love of money was idolatry. He showed her that the bursts of anger in which she had indulged were heinous sins before God, that she had totally failed in the most beautiful of all Christian virtues—filial affection; that by her greed of money she had made her husband unhappy, cruelly driven away the poor orphan Mary, and even turned away her husband's parents, those whom she ought to have cherished as if they were her own.

He showed her also that, with a fortune like hers, a little piece of bread given to a poor man to get rid of him did not fulfill the duties which God expected of her, that in spite of all her boasting of going to church she was none the better of it, for her prayers had come from a heart unwarmed by love, and could not ascend to the throne of God. In this faithful way did he talk to her, but only with the result of making her burst into a fit of passionate sobbing.

The illness from which she suffered was a long and trying one. She spent whole nights in coughing, and yet the ruling passion of avarice was so strong that she would scarcely take sufficient nourishment to sustain her. No consoling thought came to her to mitigate her suffering. She was utterly unwilling to resign herself to God and to submit to His will.

The good minister tried in every imaginable way to bring her to a better frame of mind. During the last days of her life she was occasionally a little softened in her manners, but she never evinced any true repentance. In the flower of her age she died, a sad instance of the effects of avarice, passion, and love of the world.

Chapter Twenty Two

FORGIVING AN ENEMY

And now we must return to Mary whom we left in her new surroundings.

Immediately after leaving Pine Farm, Mary went with the Count's family to the city, in which they spent part of every year. While they were there, a clergyman came one morning to their residence and asked to see Mary. He told her that he was charged with a message for her from a person who was very ill and probably near death, and who desired anxiously to speak to her. The clergyman said that the person was not willing to give her message to any one but to Mary herself.

Mary could not imagine what the woman could want with her, and she consulted the Countess as to what she ought to do. The Countess, knowing the clergyman to be a pious and prudent man, advised Mary to go with him, and at the minister's request old Anthony the huntsman accompanied them. After a long walk to the outskirts of the town, they arrived at last at a house situated in a side street, which presented a most gloomy aspect. "Here is the house," said the clergyman, knocking at the door, "but wait a little."

After a few moments he returned for Mary, who then entered with him into a most miserable room. The window was narrow and dark, and some broken panes were patched with paper. The only furniture which the room contained was a miserable trundle bed, covered with a more miserable mattress, and a broken chair, on which stood a stone pitcher, with neither handle nor cover.

On the miserable bed lay stretched a figure which to Mary's eyes seemed more like a skeleton, but which she gradually made out was the form of a woman, in the last stages of illness.

In a voice which resembled the rattle of death, this miserable creature sought to speak with Mary, who trembled in every limb. It was with the utmost difficulty that she could make out what the poor woman said, but at last she learned, to her horror, that the frightful phantom was Juliette, who at the Castle of Eichbourg had been the beginning and cause of all her distress. After being turned away from the Castle, she had gone from bad to worse, until she had sunk into her present state.

Lying upon her miserable bed, death staring her in the face, remorse had overtaken her, and her one wish was to have Mary's forgiveness. Learning in some way, that the Count and his family were in the city, she begged of the clergyman who was visiting her to ask Mary to come to see her. The poor woman, judging Mary by herself, had entreated the clergyman not to mention her name in case Mary would not come.

Mary was affected to the heart when she heard Juliette's story, and she shed tears of sympathy with her old enemy. She assured her that she had forgiven her long ago, and that the only feeling she experienced was that of the deepest pity for her.

"Alas," said Juliette, "I am a great sinner; I have deserved my fate. Forgetfulness of God, contempt of good advice, love of dress, flattery, and pleasure were the first causes of misery, and these have brought me to my present state. Oh," cried she, raising her voice to a shriek, and weeping bitterly, "that is nothing to the fate which I fear awaits me in the world to come. You have pardoned me, it is true, but I feel the weight of God's anger now settling on my soul."

Mary conversed long and earnestly with her, endeavoring to point her to the Savior of the world, who would receive her if she truly repented. At last she was obliged to leave her without being satisfied as to her state of mind, but the idea of the unhappy Juliette dying without hope continually pressed on her mind and weighed down her spirits. She recollected her little apple tree in blossom, withered by the frost, and what her father had said on that occasion. The most consoling words he had said on his deathbed presented themselves to her mind, and she renewed the promise she had made to God to live entirely to His glory.

To the Countess she related her discovery, and that generous lady sent the unhappy Juliette medicine, food, and linen, and everything which might tend to relieve her illness. But it was too late, and at the age of twenty-three the once beautiful Juliette, reduced to a mere skeleton and disfigured by disease, died without having given evidence of a changed heart towards God.

Chapter Twenty Three

MARY RETURNS TO EICHBOURG

The next spring, when the country was covered with lush greenery and fragrant flowers, the Count, accompanied by his wife, and daughter, and Mary, went to his home at Eichbourg. Towards evening they approached the village, and when Mary saw in the light of the setting sun the familiar church steeple, the Castle, and the cottage where she had spent so many happy years with her father, she was so deeply touched that tears started to her eyes.

But in the midst of the sorrowful memories which the scene called up in her mind, there came to her a devout feeling of thankfulness for the wonderful way in which God had led her back.

"When I left Eichbourg," she said, "it was in disgrace, and without ever expecting to come back again. The ways of Providence are mysterious, but God is good."

When the carriage stopped at the Castle, the servants and officers belonging to the Count's household were waiting to receive them. Mary had a warm welcome from them all. Every one showed the greatest joy at seeing her again, and their congratulations on her innocence having been proved were manifestly sincere. The old judge who had sent her into banishment hastened to be among the first to welcome the Count, that he might have an opportunity of seeing Mary also. Taking her hand in the presence of all, he asked her pardon for the injustice he had effected and telling her how deeply grieved he was to have been the unknowing instrument of all her undeserved sufferings. He expressed his gratitude to the Count and Countess for having so nobly repaired the injustice and that he was willing to do everything in his power to discharge his debt.

That night Mary could not sleep, for joy sometimes banishes sleep as well as sorrow. Early in the morning she rose, and before any of the inhabitants of the castle were awake, she set off alone to visit her old house. Even at this early hour, she met many well-known old friends, and she recognized some of the smiling young faces of the children who used to linger round her garden-gate to receive a bunch of flowers. They all looked delighted to see her again, though some of them were so grown that she scarcely knew them. Near the gate of the well-remembered garden, she saw the old farmer and his wife, who came joyfully to meet her, and welcomed her with much cordiality to her home.

"Formerly," said the old man, "when you were without a shelter, we received you under our roof, and now that we have been in a manner turned out of our home, you have given us this pleasant cottage, where we may enjoy peace and comfort in our old age."

"Yes, yes," said his wife, "one never knows how one may be rewarded for a good turn done to a neighbor."

"Come, come, wife," said the farmer, "you know we did not do it with the hope of a reward. However, the Apostle's exhortation is true in our case, 'Be not forgetful to entertain strangers; for thereby some have entertained angels unawares.' (Heb. 13:2) You have been truly an angel of mercy to us, Mary. None should ever forget the command, Use hospitality one to another without grudging.'" (1 Peter 4:9)

Mary went into the cottage with the old couple; but the sight of the home of her childhood, the corner where her father used to sit, and a number of familiar objects still remaining there awakened such sad feelings, that she could scarcely command her feelings. She went outside and walked round the garden and kissed every tree planted by her father's hand, seeing each as an old friend. The little apple tree which had been their favorite, was just now covered with blossom, and before it she stopped to meditate for a little on man's brief life, which fades away even before the tree which he has planted. In the arbor where she had passed so many happy hours with her father, she rested a little, and gave herself up to reflection. Looking around on the garden, which he had cultivated so diligently by the sweat of his brow, she fancied that she could still see him, and tears streamed from her eyes, when she remembered that he had gone from her forever. At last she recovered her composure. The remembrance of many of her father's lessons came fresh upon her mind, and raised her thoughts above the earth to the heaven which was now his home. She could not mourn for him so bitterly when she remembered how long he had been prepared, and waited patiently for his removal above, and when she recalled how often his face had beamed with rapture when he spoke to her of the heavenly inheritance, the garden of the Lord above, and of the blessedness of leaving the world, and going to be with Christ, which is far better. These recollections soothed Mary's grief; she would not have been selfish enough to call back her beloved father, even if she could have done it. She breathed an inward prayer in the accustomed spot, where she had prayed so often, that it seemed almost hallowed ground; and then taking a kind leave of the old farmer and his wife, she returned to the castle with a serene and quiet spirit.

Chapter Twenty Four

A PROPOSAL ACCEPTED

We must pass over some tranquil years, unmarked by any incident worthy of report, during which Mary remained with the young Countess as her constant companion. The Count's family lived as formerly a good deal in the town, but every spring they returned to Eichbourg, and Mary enjoyed very much the time spent there. She did not forget her old favorites the village children. The Countess Amelia accompanied her in her visits to them, and aided her in doing much good among them, both by giving necessaries of various kinds to such as required them, and by sending them to school, giving them useful books, and taking particular delight when talking to them of the Savior. She had the happiness of believing that many of them under her tutelage gave their hearts to God. The Countess and Mary would also often make little dresses and articles of clothing with their own hands, for such families as were in need.

One morning they were sitting busily engaged in making a little frock when the old judge was announced. He came in with a particularly important air, and requested a few minutes' conversation with Mary. The young Countess looked rather surprised, but immediately left the room, and left Mary to hear what he had to say. He told her that he came on behalf of his son Frederick, who had long loved and admired her, but was too good a son to tell her so, without first asking his father's consent. He added, that as soon as his son had mentioned the matter to him, he had undertaken to come up to the castle, and if Mary permitted him,

111

to speak to the Count and Countess on the subject, for as Mary was now under their protection, they were the proper people to be consulted in the matter.

Poor Mary blushed deeper and deeper while the old man spoke, and could not at first command herself sufficiently to answer him. The truth was, that she particularly esteemed the judge's son Frederick, who was really a very good young man. He was handsome and agreeable, and she had had frequent opportunities of seeing him during her annual visits to Eichbourg. She had at first been much pleased with his society; but from the moment that she had a slight suspicion that he was pleased with her, she had carefully avoided him, for she was too modest to think herself worthy of such a connection, and she wished to spare herself the pain of allowing a feeling to grow in her heart which could only serve to torment her. She had endeavored, therefore, to think as little of him as she could, and was succeeding well in rooting out every remembrance of him, when she was thus taken by surprise by his father's proposal. She blushed and grew pale by turns, and at last stammered out that she would be guided entirely by the Countess. The sharp-sighted old man guessed, by her agitation, how matters stood, and he pressed her no further, but took leave of her kindly, and sought an audience of the Countess.

The Count was with her, and the old man found both most favorably inclined to the proposal.

"I am very glad to hear what you tell us, dear sir," said the Count. We have often said that this would be a most suitable marriage. Frederick and Mary are so well suited to each other. It is not prudent to interfere in these matters, so, of course, we said nothing about it, but I have often wished that it might take place."

"I heartily congratulate you, my good friend," said the Countess; "you will gain a truly valuable daughter in Mary, and your son will have the best of wives, if she consents to be his. Mary has been taught in the school of adversity, which is the best of all. She was an admirable housekeeper, and a kind and agreeable companion before she came to us. She has shared since in all the advantages of instruction which Amelia enjoys in the town. She has acquired polished manners during her residence with us. You will find her now ladylike and accomplished, as well as amiable and good. Your son will be a fortunate man."

As soon as the Countess had heard from Mary that she was willing to consent to this marriage, she undertook most kindly to give all the necessary orders. A suitable trousseau was prepared; a marriage portion was most liberally given; and it was settled that the ring the very ring which had caused so much sorrow and so much joy—should be Mary's wedding-ring. They agreed to invite the good minister of Erlenbrünnen to officiate at the marriage.

The wedding-day turned out beautiful. All was bright and sunny. We need not dwell on the usual commonplaces of a wedding. Mary, of course, looked beautiful in her white wreath and veil; and the Countess Amelia was the prettiest and most graceful of bridesmaids. A happy crowd were present, most of whom Mary had benefited in some way or other. The old forester Anthony was present, of course, rejoicing in the happiness of his old favorite, the daughter of his oldest friend. The good minister of Erlenbrünnen officiated, and the service was most impressive.

The wedding-breakfast at the castle was as magnificent as if it had been ordered for the young Countess herself; but conspicuous above all the ornaments on the table was a basket of flowers, freshly filled by the Countess Amelia's own hands. The good minister made a special reference to it in his speech after the breakfast, and recommended that Mary should preserve it carefully as a precious heirloom, a memorial of both her trials and of her blessings.

Chapter Twenty Five

AN ENDURING MONUMENT

The telling of this charming tale could not properly be concluded without making mention of the enduring memorial to Mary's dear father James—

In due time and in fulfillment of the promise she had made to Mary the evening she had found her sitting on her father's grave, a monument was commissioned and erected to honor James. It was an elegant monument of the finest black marble, ornamented with an epitaph in gilded letters. Besides his name, age and occupation was added only these words of Jesus—

"I am the Resurrection and the Life:
He that believeth in Me,
though he were dead,
yet shall he live."
—John 11:25

Underneath these words, sculpted in bas relief from a design drawn by Amelia herself, was the perfect likeness of a basket of flowers—just as beautiful as the one first filled by Mary, and tastefully wreathed with flowers. Underneath the basket was written—

"For all flesh is as grass,
and all the glory of man as the flower of grass.
The grass withereth, and the flower thereof falleth away:
But the word of the Lord endureth forever."
—1 Peter 1:24-25

The monument gave great satisfaction to the good old minister of Erlenbrunn who had painstakingly chosen its ideal orientation within the churchyard. The verdant fir trees beyond provided a pleasant background for the monument and added to its very beautiful appearance; and when the rose bushes planted by Mary flanking the monument were in full bloom, and the branches laden with perfect roses bent to kiss the dark marble, the sight was striking. The rose blooms clustered thick and bright around the monument, but were not suffered to grow so as to hide the inscription. The black marble and the bright wreath of roses were the emblems of death, and the crown of glory to which it leads. The humble old man's monument was the most beautiful ornament of the rural churchyard, and the good minister never allowed visitors to leave the church without taking them to see it.

Whenever someone observed that it was a good idea to have put a basket of flowers on a monument to a man who had been both a gardener and a basket-maker, the old minister would say—

"Oh, but it is far better than a good idea. The basket of flowers tells more than you know, and it is not without reason that our villagers look upon it as the emblem of a poignant story—for the ground on which we tread has been bathed with a daughter's tears."

Then he would pour into the attentive ears of the strangers the charming story of the basket of flowers, concluding his recitation with the assurance which this whole story is intended to convey: That piety towards God and truth towards men will never fail to triumph over the malice of the worst of foes.

[Dear Reader, As we end our tale, it is my heartfelt prayer that its lessons leave a lasting and meaningful impression on all who have read it. If it brings good to even one soul, my effort will not have been in vain.

Let Mary's examples be a guide: she walked in reverence for God, showed love and obedience to her father, stood unwaveringly by the truth, and trusted fully in God through every circumstance. Like the beauty of flowers, her life reminds us of the beauty of simplicity, the importance of selflessness, humility and the strength found in faith.

By following these principles—seeking to live with honesty, compassion, and trust in God—you will find true happiness in this life and the assurance of eternal joy in the next. May these lessons inspire you to live a life of purpose, integrity, and hope.]

If you enjoyed
The Basket of Flowers
you'll love

Katherine "Katy" Mortimer, a naive 16-year-old consumed by vanity and romantic dreams, faces profound grief after her father's sudden death. Guided by her devout mother, she embarks on a spiritual journey, grappling with pride and temptation. Through candid diary entries, Katy transforms from self-absorption to embracing faith, discovering the beauty of a Christ-centered life filled with humility and love.

THE MISSION OF GREAT CHRISTIAN BOOKS

The ministry of Great Christian Books was established to glorify The Lord Jesus Christ and to be used by Him to expand and edify the kingdom of God while we occupy and anticipate Christ's glorious return. Great Christian Books will seek to accomplish this mission by publishing Gospel literature which is biblically faithful, relevant, and practically applicable to many of the serious spiritual needs of mankind upon the beginning of this new millennium. To do so we will always seek to boldly incorporate the truths of Scripture, especially those which were largely articulated as a body of theology during the Protestant Reformation of the sixteenth century and ensuing years. We gladly join our voice in the proclamations of— Scripture Alone, Faith Alone, Grace Alone, Christ Alone, and God's Glory Alone!

Our ministry seeks the blessing of our God as we seek His face to both confirm and support our labors for Him. Our prayers for this work can be summarized by two verses from the Book of Psalms:

"...let the beauty of the LORD our God be upon us, And establish the work of our hands for us; Yes, establish the work of our hands." —Psalm 90:17

"Not unto us, O LORD, not unto us, but to your name give glory."
—Psalm 115:1

Great Christian Books appreciates the financial support of anyone who shares our burden and vision for publishing literature which combines sound Bible doctrine and practical exhortation in an age when too few so-called "Christian" publications do the same. We thank you in advance for any assistance you can give us in our labors to fulfill this important mission. May God bless you.

Visit us for other

GREAT CHRISTIAN BOOKS

including additional titles

of fiction for young people along with

additional titles by Elizabeth Prentiss

and Maria Susanna Cummins.

www.greatchristianbooks.com

Join our email list and
receive free ebooks.